D1310234

# Dead end Kids

## HEROES OF THE BLITZ

ORCHARD BOOKS
Carmelite House
50 Victoria Embankment
London EC4Y 0DZ

This edition published in 2015 by Orchard Books

ISBN 978 1 40833 895 7

A CIP catalogue record for this book is available from the British Library.

1 3 5 7 9 8 6 4 2

Printed and bound in Great Britain by CPI Group (UK) Ltd, Croydon, CR0 4YY

Typeset in Granjon by Avon DataSet Ltd, Bidford-on-Avon, Warwickshire

The paper and board used in this book are made from wood
from responsible sources.

Orchard Books
An imprint of Hachette Children's Group,
Part of The Watts Publishing Group Limited
An Hachette UK company.

www.hachette.co.uk

# Dead end Kids

## HEROES OF THE BLITZ

ORCHARD

*This is not the true story of the famous Dead End Kids of Wapping who fought fires during the World War II Blitz. My Len Turner is not young docker Patsie Duggan, who was the real force behind the Kids' fire brigade, and Patsie's sister Maureen is not my hero Josie. The Duggans and the other Dead End Kids deserve a fitting documentary account of their bravery and sacrifices.*

*It was their story, however, that made me want to write this novel, which I have set in 'Hermitage Quays', a fictitious area of East London very loosely based on 1940s Wapping.*

*I should like to acknowledge the huge debt I owe to Anna Home, one-time head of the BBC Children's Department and currently Chair of the Children's Media Foundation. She brought the existence of the Dead End Kids to my attention and has given indispensable advice on the story and its characters.*

*B.A.*

*2015*

# 1

Josie Turner stood shouting on the deck of the old barge.

'Pugs! Mud! More ammo!'

Below her, ankle deep in sucking ooze, Shirley and Goldie bent, scooped, and threw up mud balls from the banks of Old Salt Creek. The mud was wet from the tide, but it being a hot Saturday the pugs almost dried in flight, hitting harder when they landed – which was not often because the enemy was keeping out of range.

Above Josie's Hermits gang, flying on a makeshift flagpole, was a pillowcase painted with a picture of a cowled monk carrying a lantern.

'You ain't having this barge, it's ours! Up the Hermits!' Josie pulled a defiant face for Charlie Drew and his Jubilee Boys, and for her own lot, too. But her gang would never let her down. She was a Turner and no one ever disappointed the Turners, theirs was that sort of family. She stood tall in her summer frock, brown legs and old leather sandals. Her dark hair was cut short, and her face would have been beautiful but for having her mum's hard stare, softened only by blue eyes off her dad.

That August the Hermits had prised open the hatch of the disused barge, claiming it for themselves and making the inside lively with a couple of film posters – a great place for sitting round telling spooky stories. Now the Jubilee Boys wanted what they'd got – but they weren't having it. Not a chance.

Josie threw two quick-fire pugs which fell short again. 'Yeller-bellies! Daren't come close enough!'

'Weako girl! Couldn't hit your front door from the pavement!' Charlie Drew had a cocky grin on his face.

'Shut up, Drew! You 'aven't even *got* a front door!' Josie wasn't a bit jealous of people living in Hermitage Quays' new block of council flats; let them keep their posh indoor lavs where you couldn't have a secret fag. She threw another pug but Charlie and the Jubilees were starting to creep closer in a pincer attack. She looked across the deck of the barge. Arthur Stevens was slinging pug for pug with her, just about keeping the enemy back on his side – good old Arf.

'We need longer arms to reach 'em!' He'd got mud all down his front and he'd cop it from his auntie when he went home. Her own mum might throw a clout at her, but she'd miss, she always did these days. Looking at Arthur chucking mud she reckoned she really was getting too old for all this, but when the gang said they needed her, she hadn't let them down. Well, she'd started the Hermits, hadn't she? Arthur was going to take it over – but it was a nice hot day, and she was getting to the end of her last long summer holiday before she left school at Christmas. Why not have a mud-lark with the kids? Now she was fourteen it wouldn't be long before she'd be up to her elbows in flour at the Co-op bakery every Saturday.

Charlie Drew was doing a swagger. 'We're gonna beat you, you Hermits! We're gonna capture your camp, Turner!'

'Oh, yeah?' She stood there and stared at him, dead defiant: no one ever beat Josie Turner in a no-blinking contest. But Charlie had more troops than she had, and once they broke through they'd scuttle all over the barge like cockroaches.

Arthur threw another pug, but she could see his arm was getting tired.

'Eddie! Come out of there and help!' What was the point of Eddie Rossi coming today if he was skulking inside the barge?

Eddie stuck his top half through the hatch. 'What c'n I do? Uh? I dunno what to do. Can't get dirty, can I?' He'd come out to play all clean and spoilt in his white shirt and shorts – useless!

'Come out o' there an' get throwin' cannonballs!' Saturday afternoon and here he was dressed for an Easter Parade.

'It's all dirty mud! Mama don't let me to get dirty.' Eddie shrugged his shoulders. 'I don't know it's a mud fight, coming out to play.' His father owned the Napoli café in the High Street – but being Italian he'd been taken off to a camp somewhere up north and Mrs Rossi liked Eddie looking clean around the place. Too blooming clean. Another shot fell short. Josie scooped up the next wet pug from the deck – suddenly twisting round to throw it at Eddie, catching him smack in the middle of his white shirt. *Splat!*

'You're dirty now, Ed – so come out of there an' get slingin', else we're gonna lose this war!'

'Eh!' Eddie looked down at himself, shrugged again. *'Sei ula ragazza cattiva!'* He clambered the rest of the way out of the hatch. 'So! Mud! Gimme mud!' He ran across the deck to join in the battle.

'More muscle! We're not hitting them!' Josie could see the Jubilees closing their circle tight around the barge, creeping in like the tide. If she didn't change their tactics the Hermits were going to lose the barge. But what was that, down on the bank near Shirley – something broken off a paddle?

'Shirl – sling up that bit of wood.'

She'd had an idea. Coming over here she'd seen Gummy Johnson in Victoria Gardens, and what did the old boy do when he threw the ball for his dog? He couldn't throw for toffee so he had this curvy piece of wood for slinging it a bit further.

Shirley threw the wood up for Josie to catch.

'Here you are, Arthur. Have a go with this – like

ol' Gummy. You know.' She did a quick take-off of the old man.

Charlie Drew was still looking cocky, running a couple of steps nearer. 'My men! Ready to charge!'

But Arthur was balancing the broken paddle like a slingshot, and he suddenly let loose with a double pug. *Whoosh!* They went whistling over Charlie's head, hard and fast. See him duck!

'Oi!'

Arthur's next pug hit one of the Jubilees hard in the chest, knocking him back. 'Wallop! Gotcha!'

'Good stuff, Arf! Any more of them down there, Shirl?'

Shirley found a broken spar, threw it up and Josie did the same as Arthur, shot off her next pug with spite and venom: off target, but didn't it *go*! And now the Jubilees started backing off.

'That's not fair, you lot. That's cheating!'

'No it ain't!' Arthur sent a double at the mouthy kid. 'It's superior weapons!'

Fiercely, acting the kid again and not the older girl, Josie helped the gang defend their camp, starting to re-take the ground they'd lost. 'Come on, you Hermits! We're winning! We're winning the war!' And she reckoned they were. Charlie Drew was an old enemy, had been since they'd both started school, the same age as her but younger, sort of thing: still in shorts while she was growing out of her clothes. And she could read him like a book. Any second now he'd be shouting to his men to go off and play something else.

But what she heard next wasn't Charlie Drew calling off his men. It was the air raid siren starting its growling, slowly working up to a ghostly wail before it dipped and rose like a ride on the switchback. OK, a hundred to one it was another false alarm but it was so loud no one could shut their ears to it.

'It's only ol' Moanin' Minnie. It won't be nothin'. Don't stop! We're winning!' Josie wasn't going to let some stupid shaky-hands of an air raid warden lose her Hermits their Hole.

'Pelt 'em! Save our barge!' Arthur let go with another fierce shot.

But Goldie Boston, down in the creek, was trying to wipe herself clean with tufts of grass. 'Can't fight no more, Jose. My mammy made me promise – I got to run home if the siren goes.' Goldie was younger than the others, lived with her mother along Josie's street. She was a Jamaican girl whose granddad had come to work at Wilson's Wharf as Head Horseman.

'Nah, Gold! You'll be all right with us. I'll tell your mum you was with me.' Josie Turner's say-so was good enough for anyone, wasn't it?

'She told me I've *got* to. Sorry, Jose…' Goldie pulled herself up the bank.

'Oh, don' be – some kids do have to do what their mums tell 'em.' Herself, she could twist her mother about like a stick of sucked nougat.

Goldie started running for home.

'I don't like them sirens. They make me wanna wee…' But this wasn't Goldie, it was someone wailing at the top of the bank: Patsy Riley, Jimmy Riley's little sister. Josie had seen her playing with her friends at the new flats, must have got fed up. But this was gang war, so she'd just have to wait and wail.

'Eddie – get forward! Watch out for Squib over there – cut him off with a good 'un!'

Eddie ran towards the edge of the barge, firing off mud balls with another makeshift slingshot. And with the Hermits pelting pug by pug, the Jubilees were losing and drifting away.

Josie cheered. 'Charge 'em! Charge 'em and chase 'em off!'

'Fire and conquer!'

'*Aventi!*'

'Run 'em right back to the flats!' Now Shirley was up on the bank and pelting her own pugs.

But what was that droning in the sky, getting louder and louder? All eyes went up – to where a swarm of planes was heading in from downriver, the roar of their engines making the iron barge shake.

'Jeepers!' This wasn't any nuisance raid, no couple of

planes chancing their arms. 'Help! It's only the blooming invasion!' Any second now and German soldiers were going to come parachuting out of those planes and shoot everyone to smithereens.

'Where's our army? Where's our guns?'

The planes were overhead now, so close together that their shadow darkened the ground. But it wasn't soldiers coming down.

'Bombs! They're dropping *bombs!*' Spiralling down, whistling, exploding, and sending up bursts of black smoke.

'Look at 'em all!'

'Run for your life!'

'Gas masks! We ain't got our gas masks!'

'Cover your mouths! Don' breathe!'

'Shelter!' Charlie Drew led the chase for the basement of Jubilee House across the way.

'Help! Help! I'm scared!' Patsy Riley covered her ears and cowered down.

The Jubilees ran for their shelter. Josie shouted at her gang. 'Get in the barge! In the 'Ole! Come on! It's thick as a tank!' She pulled Shirley up its side and dived through the hatch after Eddie and Arthur, slamming the cover down on top of them. But she hadn't seen how little Patsy had been left behind by Charlie Drew, scared out of her mind, her screams lost in the sounds of the bombs.

* * *

In the King George Memorial Park Len Turner's Dock Boys were drawing two-all, goal posts up but no nets: two junior teams competing in a friendly being refereed by pensioner George Knight, his trousers tucked into his socks.

Breaking up a Railway Lads' attack, Len's team came out of defence to attack down the left wing, George Knight running fast to keep up.

'Corner!' he shouted.

'Where's your whistle?' Len ran into the penalty area, jostling with the other centre-half.

'Swallered it!' George hadn't, he'd dropped it. He picked it up, blew it, and in came the corner. The hot summer had made the pitch as hard as concrete and the ball was heavy, but as it came in Len threw himself forward with a brave diving header.

'Yes!'

'Goal! Goal!'

'Good one, Len!'

'Lucky one! Come on, lads!' Clapping their hands at one another, the Railway Boys ran to take their positions for the re-start. That goal put them two-three down, and there couldn't be long to go.

'Blow for the goal, then, George!'

'Where d'you reckon you are, West Ham?' George put the whistle to his lips and sucked in a breath to

**15**

give an official blast.

But the sound they all heard wasn't his whistle; it was the start-up of the air raid siren across the park. That curdle. That wail.

'Baloney! Keep goin', won't be nothing.' The Railway Boys didn't want the match to end now. 'Don't them ARP know it's Saturday afternoon?'

But no one could ignore this new sound filling the air – and looking up they all knew the match was definitely over. The sky over East London was a dark pattern of heavy aircraft.

'God help us!'

'Get home!'

'I was goin' out, after.'

'Not no more you're not.'

'It's real!' George Knight shouted. 'Adolf's gettin' bloomin' serious!'

Len scooped up his ball from the centre-spot and began running for home. 'An' us a goal up! I'll kill that Hitler! He's ruddy started something now!'

George ran, too, doing his best to stay on his feet as the ground shook with a bomb blast. 'I was in the last lot. Started something? You can say that again, my son…'

# 2

Josie lived at number fifteen Monks Street in a dockers' house with a front door that opened onto the pavement and a cinder alley at the back, useful for a quick escape when she'd gone too far with her mother.

Ivy Turner was in the scullery getting ready for later, lining her lips with carmine – a good-looking blonde in a low-cut blouse. Tonight she'd be at the Pirate pub by the river, singing the songs people wanted to hear: 'Bye-bye Blackbird', 'All of Me', 'Smoke Gets in Your Eyes', and 'We'll Meet Again' – a local performer with a touch of class. She was Ivy to everyone, even to Josie and Len in their heads. She stopped her lip-lining as the sound of the Wilson's Wharf air raid siren broke in on her – pulling a face into the mirror for the ARP fool who'd plonked his mug of tea on the warning button. But the wailing went on at full blast, and with it there was a deeper droning getting louder and louder.

'Oh my God, what's that?'

A sudden great boom rattled the windows and shook the house.

'Josie! Lenny!' Ivy threw down her make-up and ran to the front door. '*Josie!*' she shouted in a voice to rival the raid.

People from both sides of the street were running

from their houses, heading towards the river for the public shelter in the basement of Wilson's Wharf.

'Shelter! Get down the wharf!'

'Ivy! Come on, girl! Shelter!' Emma Varley from next door showed a good turn of speed for a pensioner.

'How can I, Em? My Josie's out in this! And Lenny!'

Lou Sutton from the local pictures came running by. 'Ivy – get yourself down that shelter!'

'Can't. Josie! You seen my Josie?'

Lou drew breath. In her early sixties she wouldn't normally run for anything. 'No, but that girl's got her head screwed on. She's not a kid no more – she'll get herself somewhere safe.'

'And Lenny's over the park!'

'Yeah, with my George. But there's a shelter over there…'

A girl was running past – Goldie from down the street. 'Goldie! Goldie Boston! You seen my Josie?'

But Goldie ran on fast, screaming in the aircraft drone as she stretched for home.

'*Josie!* Lord help us! Josie, you little cat, where are you?'

Another explosion shook the ground, closer this time, the blast taking slates off roofs and breaking windows.

*Shelter! Shelter! Shelter!* The word was all over, taken up by Air Raid Warden William Bailey, running past.

'Shelter! Get to the shelter, Mrs Turner!'

'My kids! I'm not going nowhere without my kids!'

Warden Bailey blew his whistle into Ivy's face. 'Look to yourself, woman. You're no good to your kids if you're dead.' He ran on towards the shelter, overtaking Lou Sutton, who was behind Goldie as she got nearer to her house – when suddenly the air was filled with a loud, scary whistling.

'Take cover! High Explosive Bomb!' Warden Bailey started running for the girl. Ivy ducked and Lou braced herself against a wall. A searing flash obliterated everything; the blast knocked everyone off their feet: the street was thrown up and back down as smoke, cordite, and brick dust stung eyes and clogged throats. And as the air slowly began to clear, Goldie's house was now no more, just a mound of rubble and blazing woodwork, the worst off of three stricken buildings.

And there was nothing to be seen of Goldie.

'Blimey – look at this!' Josie's head was out of the hatch staring up at the bombers still coming over, line after line of large aircraft with RAF fighters nipping in and out at them like wasps. Puffs of smoke in the sky showed where the ground guns were aiming, and in the creek the air was filled with the smell of mouldy clay, cooking gas and sulphur.

'Josie!' She heard a scream, and there was little Patsy Riley in a huddle on the bank.

'Pats! What you doin' out there?'

'I'm gonna be killed!'

'No you ain't. You're coming in the 'Ole with me…' Josie jumped from the barge and ran across to pull at Patsy's arm. This was Jimmy Riley's little sister and she needed looking after, for herself, and on behalf of Jimmy. The Rileys lived a street away from them and Jimmy's mother would be going mad wanting Patsy safe down a shelter. She gave the girl a leg up the side of the barge and dropped her down to Arthur. 'Cop hold of Patsy!'

'It's dark!'

'Iron barge, Pats, they don' have windows. Thick old party, though. You're OK now, girl. You're safe as houses in here.'

But screaming little Patsy didn't look at all convinced. She shivered and shuddered. 'I want my ma!'

Hermitage Quays and its Eastern and Western docks were being hit hard, and along the Thames from North Woolwich to Tower Bridge flames flew up from warehouses and factories, timber stacks and oil tanks. Rows of small houses dominoed down, and from all over London, Essex and Kent hundreds of fire pumps raced for the East End docklands. In half an hour London had gone from sunny afternoon to choking pall.

Stepney Street Elementary School was now an Auxiliary Fire Station and Ambulance Centre. It had two bungalow buildings. One now belonged to the AFS with its fire engines and motorcycle messengers. The other was a First Aid dressing station and the control HQ for ambulances. Classrooms were now firemen's, nurses', and drivers' sleeping quarters. The headmaster's office was the watch-room, and the playground was parking space for fire engines and St John ambulances.

Station Officer Ralph Wiltshire was standing in the watch-room with Firewoman Fleming sitting at the telephone switchboard. Wiltshire was speaking on his phone extension as he watched the last of his fire appliances – a London taxi pulling a small pump – drive out through the school gates.

'That's the bally last of 'em.' Station Officer Wiltshire had risen from being a Barnardo's Boy orphan and normally spoke with more care to District Control. 'You do know, don't you – we're taking a right packet over here? Never seen anything like it. I need at least ten pumps for back-up – anything you've got. The whole ruddy world's ablaze.'

Joyce Fleming tore a scribbled sheet off her pad – another call-out.

''Scuse my French,' Wiltshire told her, 'but they should've known this was goin' to happen. Stands to reason. Where's anyone going to want to hit London? In the bread basket – the docks...'

Urgent buzzers sounded on the switchboard.

'How the devil can I send out what I haven't got? Who do they think I am? The Wonderful Wizard of Oz?'

A grey fire engine raced along Monks Street, swerving around debris and stopping as near as it could to the ruins of Goldie's house. One wall was partly standing, the rest of it was a pile of rubble and burning floorboards and rafters. Lou Sutton and a party of neighbours were pulling at hot bricks as bits of scorched curtain blew about like frantic bats.

Lou ran to the fire engine. 'There was a kiddie running down here. She's either under this lot or blown to smithereens. I see her, just before it hit.' She coughed up brick dust, wiped her streaming eyes.

'Keep digging – till we get some rescue boys here.' The Leading Fireman was already at the tap-wheels of the pump. 'Just watch out for that dodgy wall.'

A quick look up at the sky and Lou ran back to shift more bricks. Two firemen connected an inlet hose to a hydrant in the street; two others unrolled an outlet hose from the pump to the burning timbers.

'Right, lads. Let's knock this fire down. All ready?'

The firemen raised their hands.

'On my command – engage pump!'

The hydrant key was turned, the pump's engine rose to full throttle, the outlet opened and the hose fattened with water, the two men at the nozzle wrestling to direct a jet at the burning rafters on either side of the stricken house. The sky was black with smoke and red with flames; above, German bombers droned over endlessly. The Leading Fireman waved up at the sky and at the whole East End. 'We're squirting water pistols at a bloomin' volcano.'

'Yeah – an' with a little kiddie gone up in the ashes!' Lou shouted. 'Bloody rotten Hitler!'

# 3

The Hermit Hole had an oil drum for a table, with a couple of broken chairs and a stool. Everything was at a slight angle where the barge was stuck up a bank. Josie had daubed 'Hermits' in tar on the inside plating, next to an old poster from the Globe Cinema – the Bowery Boys in *Dead End*. An iron ladder led up to the hatch, propped open right now for air and a shaft of light. But what filled the barge was noise – the sounds of the bombs exploding in the docks and streets, their impact vibrating through the iron hull.

Josie and the others sat huddled, fingers in ears, eyes tight-closed against falling rust – and with Patsy Riley still crying.

'Oh, shut up, Patsy!' Josie could do without her going on. 'You're all right down here. This thing's got iron a mile thick. We're not goin' to get killed in here, are we, Arf?'

''Course not.' Arthur cringed with the rest as another explosion rattled around the hull. 'But I will when I get home.'

'We all will.' Josie didn't know much about Arthur's real home where his mum lived, he never said anything about that; but everyone knew he lived with a very strict auntie who'd got a cane called 'Uncle Jack'.

'She'll skin me alive. I was only s'posed to go to the shops when Drew let on what he was up to…'

'Tell her you'd have only broke her eggs. You saved her the money.' Josie was darned if she was going to take the blame for Arthur getting into the barge war. He'd seen her in the street, told her about Charlie Drew's plan to capture the Hermit Hole, and she'd decided to help them out. She'd got other things she'd rather be doing today, thanks, and she wasn't going to land in trouble for a bit of fun with the old gang.

'I bet my mum's going potty over me.' Shirley pulled a scared face that started Patsy crying again.

'An' me. My mama's gonna think I'm dead.' Eddie cut his throat with his finger.

'Well, you ain't.' Josie shrugged. 'An' what they think's not our fault. They'll all be going potty, but no one was kept indoors by their mums, was they? The government never sent no message not to let kids go out to play, did they?'

With a street-flattening explosion another bomb fell somewhere close, its blast pulling the barge from the suck of the mud, sending rust and rivets showering down – as near a miss as anything yet.

Patsy screamed her head off. 'I'm gonna die. I want my ma!'

Josie grabbed her for a quick cuddle. She could see Mrs Riley's face – skinny, worrying whether or not to leave her other kids to go chasing out looking for Patsy.

The crumbled remains of a fairy cake were on the oil drum. 'Here y'are, Pats. Get this down you, chewing'll deaden the sound.'

Still wailing, Patsy took the cake and put it into her mouth, turning the paper cup inside out to get to the last crumbs.

'Gawd, you was hungry!'

'Always...am...' – which ended in hiccups and fractured wailing.

The blast of the last bomb was still shaking the barge. 'We're gonna get killed in here. I'm going home!' Shirley was heading for the ladder.

But Josie beat her to it. 'Yeah – come on, everyone out! Duck your heads down low an' run for the shelter.'

Eddie looked in a dither. 'You said it was safe down here.'

'Ever been wrong, 'ave you?' Josie climbed the ladder, opened the hatch full up and looked out again. 'Jeepers!' She'd never seen so much smoke, it dropped her mouth open, dried it out. 'Come on, Pats!' She pulled her out, jumped her off the barge and started running for Wilson's Wharf – around rubble, over broken slate and glass, through thick smoke and floating sparks. 'Help us! What's gonna be left after this lot?' And what would be left of them: herself, Ivy, Len – and Jimmy Riley? And as she ran she did something unusual for her. She said a prayer. 'Save us, God! Save us all!' And then, 'Come on, Patsy, move them feet for Chrissake!'

The posters at the Globe Cinema were advertising the Dead End Kids in *Crime School*, but right now the foyer was chained shut as George Knight ran for the old stage door at the side.

'Lou! Lou! You down there?' George opened up. No reply. Len Turner had run with him this far, but he was all for getting on to Wilson's Wharf. George turned to him. 'Be stupid if she's in the flat but I'm gonna check. You get yourself yourself down the shelter.'

'See you, George. If I see Lou I'll tell her you ain't dead – yet!' Len ran on with quick looks up, as if he could ever dodge a bomb coming down. He ran three more streets but as he rounded the last corner he saw something that pulled him up short. The stables near the wharf were on fire, with old Elijah Boston squirting water from a hosepipe up at the roof – a fight he wasn't winning.

'Where's Jimmy?' Jimmy Riley was stable lad and ought to be with Elijah, helping.

'Jimmy's inside. Stopping them beasts from kicking the stalls to mish-mash.'

'Can't you get 'em out?'

'Then what? More'n twenty of them, they'll charge

all over the place from Timbuktu to the Barbary Coast. See if I can beat this first.'

'Well, you got no chance on your own.' Len took a deep breath and ran into the stables where Jimmy Riley and Ellie the stable lass were trying to calm the frightened beasts – shire horses rearing up with their mouths foaming, their teeth bared, their eyes flashing. Smoke was drifting down from the roof; but Len could see through it to the bales of feed and the wooden stalls. 'God Almighty, Jimmy. If this lot goes up you're in dead trouble!'

'Steady, Duke boy, steady on.' Jimmy was patting a huge shire, talking to it head-to-head.

Len saw where Elijah's hose was connected to one of two taps. He threw out the bran from a bucket and kicked it under the free tap. 'You all right, Jimmy? 'Cos that fire's winning up there.'

'Lucky it lodged there and didn't drop into the bedding.' Jimmy ran to a stall at the far end, where a sleek grey was whinnying and kicking. 'Easy, Topper, go easy, boy.' He stroked down the horse's nose and whispered into its ear. 'It's all goin' to be all right, my beauty.'

At last Len's bucket was full. He found another and pushed it under the tap. Jimmy left Topper and snatched up a stirrup pump from a corner of the tack room. 'Grab a hold of this. I'll follow out, quick as I can.' He shouted down to Ellie. 'Keep on sweet-talking. Kiss 'em. Promise 'em anything.'

Len ran out with the full bucket and the stirrup pump and set them down next to Elijah.

'Sweet Lord, Leonard, what sins have we committed to bring this down upon us-selves?'

Len knew stirrup pumps, he'd been trained in the docks. He pushed the stirrup flat to the ground with his foot, steadied the pump, and with one hand pumping he aimed the hose up at the fire. A good strong effort could send the water thirty feet.

'Keep it high, Elijah, in under the slates! It's getting thick as pea soup in there.'

But something had turned Elijah's head – the bells of a fire engine, racing along Wharf Road.

'Hallelujah, boy! Here comes the Admiralty!'

But the fire engine didn't stop. It went ringing on past them.

'Thank you, gen'lmen.' Elijah shook his fist. 'You turn your blind eyes!'

The fire engine reached the junction with Tamask Street, where Warden Bailey was waving it towards the Western Dock.

'Then it's still you an' me, boy!'

Len pumped on fiercely, almost emptied the bucket – and was about to throw its dregs up at the flames when Warden Bailey came running at him, hampering his throw.

'Watch out, Mr Bailey!'

'What're you doing here, son?'

'Playing Jack and Jill. What do you think I'm doing?'

'Kids like you shouldn't be out in this.' He looked up at the fire. 'Incendiary bomb in the roof space. Leave it to the adults.'

'You mean adults like that grown-up fire engine that's just gone steaming past?'

'Don't be cheeky, son, an' get down the shelter!'

Jimmy came running out with two full buckets. Len ignored Warden Bailey, took one of Jimmy's buckets and pushed his pump into it – but Bailey was trying to take it from him. 'I'll handle this.'

They tussled, but Len was stronger than Warden Bailey; if it came to a fight it would be no contest. He hit the flames again.

'Get down that shelter with the other kids.' Warden Bailey pulled hard at Len's arm – which Len suddenly allowed to give, twisting the hose and giving the man a good squirt in the face.

'Oi! You little…'

'Oop! Sorry, mate!'

Turning his back on Warden Bailey, Len went on fighting the fire while Jimmy ran in and out with buckets. At last the smoke was beginning to thin. 'We're winning, Elijah!'

'I do believe we are, Leonard.'

'Two squirts are better than one!'

'I've got people to look after.' Warden Bailey looked as if he wasn't sure where to go or what to do. 'But these juveniles should be taking cover.'

'An' I'm almighty grateful they aren't, Mr Bailey. They've both started work, haven't they? An' if they're old enough to work, they're old enough to save my stable.'

Len switched buckets again, pointing the hose for a second at Warden Bailey, who backed off. 'A war's a war, Mr Bailey, in case you didn't know. An' we're all in it. Germans don't make their bombs so they miss the kids, do they? You think about that.' And he started pumping again until the roof was finally dampened down.

'God bless you, Leonard.'

Jimmy Riley snorted. 'An' what about God blessing the likes of me an' Ellie?'

'You don' count, Jimmy boy. You're paid to be here!' With a chuckle Elijah ruffled the Irish boy's hair. 'But them beasts are almighty grateful.'

Len looked at the smoking wooden stables. 'All that hay and straw. If we hadn't been sharpish them horses would've been either dog food or running all over London. An' all down to one little devil of an incendiary bomb!'

\* \* \*

Lou was grabbing at bricks in the wreckage of Goldie's house. The fires on either side had been put out and the fire engine had gone.

'No sign of anyone.' Fred Bowyers eased his back. He was an elderly neighbour of the Bostons from over the road. 'I don't reckon she's under here at all. If you ask me, the poor little blighter's a goner. Blown to smithereens…'

'Looks hopeless.' Lou straightened up; with bombs still falling all around she looked half ready to leave this and get herself to the shelter. 'And if the woman was in the house she's down under these bricks – an' dead as a doornail.' Explosions reverberated up and down the river and oily smoke from the docks was spreading across the sky like black paint. 'Hello! What's this?' Josie Turner was running down the street with some other kids. 'Your mum's going barmy looking for you!'

Josie grabbed at a lamppost to make a quick stop. She'd just run past burning buildings and around gas-leaking holes in the road, her ears had been blasted, her eyes smoked, her legs and arms hit by flying glass splinters. 'Not our fault the siren went!' But leave that. She was taking in the brick-dust and devastation of where this house had been. 'Hold up! This is near Goldie's place!'

'This *is* Goldie's place. That's her lamppost!' Shirley put her knuckles to her mouth. 'Little Gold! She should've stayed with us.'

Lou stood up on a heap of rubble. 'You kids get down the shelter!'

'Was Goldie here? Did she get home?'

Lou pointed up at the planes in the sky, another wave coming over. 'Just get away, all of you!'

'I told her to stay with us. I told her to stay with us.' Josie had to get this straight for everyone. 'She should've stayed with us. Anyhow, come on, you lot. If there's half a chance she's under here we're gonna help.' She ran onto the rubble and started pulling at bricks.

Eddie hesitated. 'What about my mama?'

'What about my auntie?' But Arthur was already stooping to help. 'Goldie's a Hermit.'

'We need Ace the Wonder Dog.' Shirley climbed the rubble, too.

'You're good kids. Good mates.' Lou looked up at the sky. 'It's gone quiet for a bit. Get stuck in, then.' She went back to moving bricks with the other neighbours. 'But, careful where you tread. Keep yourselves light. One of 'em might be right under where you're standing.'

Eddie gave a little jump.

Josie chose a mound of bricks away from Lou and the others. She didn't know what she'd do if she saw a hand, or an arm poking out – or, God help her, a head – but she knew they'd got to do this until they couldn't do it any more. She was responsible. Goldie was Goldie, and like Arf said, a Hermit was a Hermit.

A sudden scream stopped her. She'd forgotten Patsy – who was standing a yard from the pavement, pointing across the street.

Shirley had seen what Patsy had, and shrieked. Arthur had seen it, and howled. Eddie had seen it, too, and shouted, '*Fantasma!*'

All the digging stopped. Everyone stood and stared. There on the opposite pavement was a girl the same shape and size as Goldie; but this girl was a deathly white all over, looking every bit like something walking out of a grave.

'It's Goldie's ghost!'

The girl in white slowly drifted across the street towards them, hands outstretched, doing her own weird wailing as the Hermits backed further up the rubble.

Shirley shivered and hugged herself. 'Goldie's got killed – and her ghost's come to haunt us!'

'She's dead an' coming for us...' And Arthur usually talked sense.

'Jeepers!' But Josie stood her ground. 'Don't be little kids! There's no such things as ghosts.'

The sight kept on coming, step after step. Arthur jumped off the bombed site. 'Come on, you lot, shelter!' But Josie walked towards the sight. She held out her hand. 'Gold! You're alive!' She looked into the dark eyes staring from the white face.

'What...happened...?'

'Dunno. But you'll soon be our Goldie again.' She started dusting the girl down.

Lou ran across the road and picked Goldie up. 'Come on, love, let's get you seen to, eh?'

Josie left her in Lou's good hands and ran with the others to take cover in the basement of Wilson's Wharf.

Which was when it suddenly hit her what war really meant. Not mud and pugs but bombs and deaths and being scared and bloody angry. And you didn't grow up bit by bit in a war, it could happen in a day.

# 4

Arthur's aunt was already in the shelter, and when Josie and the Hermits went in she gave Arthur a good clip around the ear. 'I'm not letting you out of my sight till England's won this war!'

It was a teeth-grinding time as Shirley and Eddie asked neighbours where their mothers were. But after half an hour Mrs Rossi came rushing in, eyes darting all around. When she saw her boy she shrieked, wept, kissed him and clutched his muddy middle to her stomach. Shirley's mother came in and went to pieces like Bette Davis in a Hollywood weepie, and Arthur's aunt gave him another clip round the ear for drifting six inches away. Meanwhile, Josie mothered Patsy Riley – until Father Wearden came in to tell the girl to stay where she was: the rest of her family were safe in the crypt of St Patrick's Church.

'See – they'll be all right, Pats, an' you're all right down here.'

Len seemed shocked to see Josie. 'I thought you was with Ivy somewhere.'

'No.' She saw his blackened face. 'Where was you?'

He told her about the stables fire.

'Is…are the horses all right? Like Topper.' Wherever Topper was, that's where Jimmy Riley would be – the

Irish boy who let her groom the white horse; the Wilson's Wharf stable lad with the touch of blarney that sometimes turned her cheeks red.

'All all right there, Jose. Horses, Ellie, Jimmy, Elijah, up to when I came down.'

'Oh, my God!' *Elijah!* He was Goldie's granddad. She told Len about Goldie's house and Lou taking Goldie home to the Globe.

''Strewth! I'll get along there an' see if he knows—' just as Warden Bailey came into the shelter; and when he saw Len he went for him.

'Lenny Turner – never you mind what Elijah Boston was saying – kids like you are a blooming nuisance, getting in the way. I'm properly trained. Two years of nights I've done getting ready for this lot – and I don't want you kids playing at war on my patch.'

Len wanted away, but he stood and laughed in the warden's face. 'Two years' training for squirting a stirrup pump? Get off! You *need* the likes of me! You saw that fire engine go steaming past. You'd be looking all over the East End for twenty horses if I hadn't helped put that fire out. An' I tell you, mate – when I see flames I'm gonna do the self-same thing again.'

Micky the shelter warden came over to calm things, and Len made to get off to see Elijah. But coming through the doorway was Ivy.

'Len! Thank God you're safe! I'm going frantic.

Frantic!' She clutched him, hugged him, ruffled his smoky hair. 'Where's Josie? You seen that girl?'

'She's all right. She's over there.'

Ivy let him go, stared around. 'Josie Turner!' She pushed her way through the shelter as if she was going to flatten the girl – and gave her the biggest cuddle in the world, a hug that hurt. 'Thank God! Thank God! I've been all over looking for you!' Ivy didn't cry, she rarely did, but Josie knew from the husk in her throat she wasn't far off it. 'Where were you?'

'The kids wanted me to help them fight Charlie Drew. I didn't know this lot was going off, did I?'

'Why didn't you run home, you silly cat?'

''Cos I ran here.' There was no answer to that. She thought.

'I checked in here first.' The fold of her arms and the tilt of her head said Ivy hadn't been brought up on a winkle barge.

But she didn't need to know the Hermits had been risking their lives under the bombs looking for Goldie. 'It's a big place. I was probably having a wee.' Josie pointed to the hospital screens that hid the buckets.

'Well, you ain't going out of my sight from now on. So just make yourself small an' behave yourself.'

It was the worry, Josie knew. Mums worried tons worse than dads. She gave her a hug back. 'Anyhow, I'm glad you're OK yourself.'

'Yeah. All right.' And Ivy smiled, a smile that started off as reassurance but finished with her eyes filling up. 'Find somewhere to sit, for Gawd's sake, and be good.'

Josie sat on the floor. Wilson's Wharf basement was hardly ready for an air raid. Hitler had caught everyone out: there weren't enough chairs, the lavatory was the two screens rigged up in front of two buckets, one for men, one for women, and when a bomb fell close by and the lights went out, the oil lamps could only glimmer in the gloom. Everyone was scared and ratty. After another half-hour of bombs sending shock waves through the concrete, Ivy tried to get a sing-song going; but she was told to leave it – they needed a piano and a pint for that sort of thing.

Suddenly the place was shaken by a really close explosion. It came through the floor, swung the lights, took whitewash off the walls. Everyone ducked their heads, and cried, and prayed, and went on about how nothing could save them if they got a direct hit.

Josie was scared with the rest. And what had happened to Goldie had been close. She knew about death; she'd known kids who'd died – Maureen Black at school, taken off with diphtheria; Johnnie Comber, drowned in the Eastern Dock; and Lucy Reading's little sister who'd stood too close to the kitchen fire in her fairy dress. But Goldie from along their street was like family – and Goldie's mum wasn't just a name in Warden Bailey's book, she was a real person who passed their house every day with her shopping bag and her winter coat, even in the summer. And her favourite saying was: 'Nice day for everything, don't you think?' Well, it wasn't, today.

The air raid came and went and came back again. It would be quiet for twenty minutes with everyone listening out for the All Clear, but more planes would come droning over instead and it would all start up again.

'Go out an' shout up at 'em, Micky-boy – tell the blighters they've made their point, enough's enough.'

But Micky preferred to stick to what he was doing, minding the blackout, trying to make the old folk comfortable, shifting feet off seats, and shaking a bottle of Dettol behind the lavatory screens; until things went really quiet, and finally there it was – the All Clear, with everyone crowding the doorway to get away, dark thoughts surfacing.

'Gawd – wonder what's happened to my place…?'

'If Hitler's cracked my Toby jugs…'

'I daren't look. I dread turning that corner…'

'I bet I'll never see that cat again. They know, animals…'

The Turners had got off lightly. Len patched up a couple of broken windows, Josie beat ceiling plaster out of the rugs, and Ivy made the beds again before putting some tea on the table.

Josie waited for her moment to ask – by way of telling. 'Think I'll shoot down the stables an' see how them horses are. That Topper's a real nervy case…'

But Ivy wasn't having it. 'You're sticking indoors, my girl. What if a gas main goes up? Or a wall falls on you? It's not just bombs that kill people.'

Josie knew when she had a chance of winning, and when she was on a loser – and after that raid today Ivy seemed set as hard as concrete; it wasn't worth wasting words. She sat and looked at the picture of her dad on the mantelpiece. She could always wheedle him: Private Turner, First Battalion the Essex Regiment, cap on, khaki collar up, and a grim mouth like 'I'm coming to get you, Hitler!' Except he didn't fool her. The look in his eyes told her he was an old softie who was missing them all like mad. But 'softie' never came into it with Ivy, so Topper – and Jimmy Riley – would have to wait.

Her stomach froze over as the air raid siren wailed again.

'I don't believe it! Half eight. I've only just drawn breath!' Ivy grabbed what she'd put ready for the next day – her handbag with house keys and rent book and a small bottle of gin; cushions, blankets and a welfare orange juice. She chased Josie and Len out of the house, the three of them running back to Wilson's Wharf with the sounds of heavy aircraft dashing any hopes of it being a false alarm.

'The blighters!'

They bombed on for eight and a half hours until the sunrise sent them back. But in the middle of it, in all the squeeze and the discomfort, Warden Bailey came through the shelter door and looked out old Mr Bowyer from along their street.

'They dug your neighbour out, Fred, but she's in a coma, more dead than alive, I'm sorry to say…'

Josie wasn't one for praying, but she turned away and shut her eyes for the second time that day. 'Thank you, God, for not letting Goldie run home any quicker.' She looked over at where Ivy was sharing a drop of gin with Auntie Varley from next door. A load of grief in the house, mums were, but wouldn't it be terrible if she copped one like poor Mrs Boston?

Len was up and out of the house early, Josie didn't know where. It was Sunday, he wasn't meant to be working, unless he'd been suddenly called into the docks. But he could be a real tight-mouth when he wanted. She waited until Ivy was upstairs sticking strips of brown paper to the windows, then she scooted out of the door.

'Jeepers!'

She was in a different world. Down her street, along by the wharves, up by the Western Dock – Hermitage Quays was a battered place. It smelt like Guy Fawkes Night, ash floating in the air, slate and glass crunching under her feet, and roads turned to a different colour where the undersides of cobbles were facing the sky. Everyone seemed to be out of doors. There were tarpaulins being stretched over missing roofs; broken bits and pieces covered the ground – with done-for ornaments being picked over and swept up, and bowls of water being sloshed on the pavements for God-knew-what to be scrubbed away.

'Look at that dinner service. Thirty years I've had them plates. Bone china.'

'Thirty years I've had my husband. Bone idle.'

A bit of a laugh in the middle of everything; but Josie saw teams of men in steel helmets digging for bodies on the bombed sites – Baxter's Wharf, Solomons' Candle Works; and she walked past totally demolished houses, in one street a row of them all gone down together. Firemen were still running out their hoses and dousing fires, sending up wet grey smoke; and across the sky above the docks was a black curtain of cloud where oil was still blazing. She saw an elderly, dazed-looking couple walking in the middle of the road, peering from side to side as if they were searching for something; and a man wrapped in a blanket standing staring at the smashed front of a tea room, tears running down his face. And she saw bombed-out families with heaped-up prams pushing their way out of Hermitage Quays. She passed a house that was half sliced-off, leaving a fireplace

**43**

clinging to the wallpaper of a bedroom that wasn't there any more.

'She never stood a chance, poor old duck.'

And Josie knew who that was – old Mother Breadcrumbs, who used to walk the streets feeding the birds with crumbs out of her pockets, whistling them down from the roofs through her snaggy teeth. Well, that was one crackers old girl who wouldn't get teased any more.

'Scarper, girl, 'less you want to see sumthin' you don' want to see.' Along by the wharves, down by the Thames, up by the bridges to the docks, whichever way she turned she was shooed off in case she saw something horrible.

'You ought to be away, evacuated.'

'This ain't for kids! Off out of it, miss!'

She headed for the Hermit Hole to see if it had got through the night – and to check that Charlie Drew and the Jubilee Boys hadn't captured it. It wouldn't bother her too much today, although Arthur and the others would be upset. She needn't have worried. The barge was all in one piece with the Hermit flag still flying. Across the way, the Jubilee Buildings people were doing their own sweeping up: on the balconies, down on the pavement and in the road; every window in the block must have been broken. She saw where Patsy Riley had been huddled on the bank, the battered door of a council van sticking up out of the ground on that very spot. But thinking of Patsy made her think of Jimmy, who'd be at the stables – and a little twitch in her veins somehow told her she was going to end up there today, helping him with Topper.

Before that, though, there was someone else she needed to see, alive and talking: Goldie, who'd been taken by Lou to the Globe. But around the next corner at Empire Tobacco she was stopped by the sight of a fireman four storeys up, swaying about at the top of a ladder, steam coming off his wet uniform. 'Oh, my God!' It was like something out of Sanger's circus: any second he was going to get thrown off his ladder and go dropping down into the burning building. The turntable on top of the fire engine was swinging the ladder left then right above the flames as the fireman did his best to get the nozzle of his hose in line with a loading bay. But the ladder finally steadied, and the hose jet started hitting its target. She opened her mouth to give him a cheer when the sound of a motorbike turned her around. But it wasn't the motorbike that took her eye, it was the girl who was riding it: snazzy, smart, in a Fire Brigade uniform – boots, large gauntlets and a jaunty cap. The girl got off her bike and ran to the fireman in charge of the pump. She pulled a piece of paper from a pouch on her belt. The fireman read the message, screwed it up, and shoved it into his tunic pocket.

Josie edged closer.

'What does he think we are? Ruddy robots? My boys haven't had a minute's sleep, they've barely sipped at a cup of tea since four o'clock yesterday.'

'Yes, sir. Will I report that back?' She was Scotch by the sounds of her.

'No, dammit, I'll tell him myself. You can say we'll get to the next shout as soon as we've knocked this one down, but we're returning to the station after that. Exhausted men can't fight fires, they're not safe to.'

'Yes, sir.' The dispatch rider offered a small pad and a pencil.

'Just tell him.'

'Sir.' The girl pulled her motorbike – a Matchless – off its stand, mounted it, gave it a kick-start, and was off, weaving her way around the rubble in the road.

Josie watched her go, her chest filling with the sight of that messenger in a smart uniform. Just the sort of thing for her! Right up her street. She looked down at herself. She was getting tall, filling out, didn't look or feel like a kid any more, she could twist a wet sheet nearly as dry as Ivy could. And she was leaving school at Christmas. On Sundays she'd used to go over to Epping Forest on the back of her dad's AJS and he'd let her have a go on her own. She could ride a Matchless all right, no problem. So, at what age did the fire brigade take their messengers?

What had happened yesterday and what she'd seen

this morning seemed to have been leading her somewhere. To this. She'd found out what war was about. And now she knew what she wanted to be about herself. As soon as she could, she was definitely going to have some of that messenger stuff.

# 5

The Globe Picture House in Thomas Street had once been a music hall. The great Marie Lloyd had played there, and top comedian Max Miller. But for some time it had been a 'third run' cinema, showing older films seen first time around at plush places like the Troxy in Commercial Road. People could go to the Globe three times a week and see something different each time, while for the youngsters it had Saturday Morning Pictures. But it wasn't a 'flea pit'; it was well run by Harry Knight, whose brother George was second projectionist and caretaker, and had Lou Sutton as queen of the ticket kiosk.

Josie didn't get as far as Lou's and George's flat. Checking on Goldie wasn't going to happen just yet because when she arrived George was in the foyer sweeping up broken glass, and before she could ask to go downstairs he'd swept her towards the inside doors.

'In you go, girl.'

'What?' Josie hadn't come to see any film – jeepers, they weren't doing Saturday Morning Pictures on a bombed-out Sunday, were they? Anyway, she was too old for all that.

'Your Len's in there, and the rest. Shift yourself, you're late.'

*Len?* What was he doing here? She went inside, where under the cleaners' lights the screen looked flat and dead; but up in front of it stood a very alive Len. He was making a speech to two or three rows of kids, pointing at them from time to time with the short iron bar he'd been given by their granddad when he'd retired from the docks.

'We can help, an' we're gonna help. I'm as strong as Bill Bailey, stronger. If I blew on him I'd have him flat on his bum. I can pump a stirrup a darned sight faster than he can, and so can a lot of you…'

The kids cheered. Bill Bailey wasn't just a bossy air raid warden – his day job was in the rent office where he was well known for his hard edge. Asking him for a week's leeway on your mother's rent was like banging your head on the side of a sink.

'Them Jerries'll be coming back, we all know that, they're saying so on the wireless, an' it'll probably be tonight. An' we all saw it yesterday – the poor old fire brigade's all over the place, trying to be at a million fires at once. They're still out there now, an' they will be, all day.'

Josie sat herself at the end of an empty row. She looked at the kids in front of her – some who'd already left school like Len, some who hadn't, and she knew every one of them.

'So we're gonna help. An' this is what we're gonna do…'

Tony Milner clapped. 'About time! Get on with it, Len!'

Josie knew Len would have flattened Tony Milner out in the street, but this wasn't her brother Len up there, making a speech on a stage. He was a general. He pointed his iron bar at Milner. 'What we're gonna do, Milner, is we're gonna start up our own fire brigade – all people like us who can handle stirrup pumps, throw sand on Hitler's fireworks, chop our way through doors, an' get old ladies out of their beds an' down the shelters…'

'Young ladies an' all, Len. I'll 'elp with the young 'uns!'

Josie leant over the seat in front and slapped Willy Fraser round the head. 'Not me, you won't!'

'We'll get hold of barrers, carts, prams, buckets, bits of hose, hammers, shovels, the sort of gear the firemen's got, all that paraffin-alia, an' when we see a fire, 'specially incendiaries, we'll handle it ourselves an' let the fire brigade get on with the big stuff.' Len waved his iron bar at them again, row by row. 'It's gonna be proper organised, not everyone chasing their arse all over the shop. I've worked it out.' Tucking the bar under his arm he pulled a scruffy piece of paper from his trouser pocket. 'In teams, it'll be, with a leader to each team an' four or five men with a barrer each, an' a stirrup pump, an' all the stuff we need.'

Josie sat there, her mouth open. When had he worked all this out? But, whenever, it was a blooming good idea.

'Where we gonna get all the stuff, Len?' someone shouted.

Josie saw a few heads shaking at this ignorance – kids who knew darned well where they'd get what they wanted. And she knew, too – out of sheds, from backyards, tool-chests, cupboards under the stairs, scullery drawers, all sorts of places at home – or they'd nick it, pilfer it, half-inch it, have it away when people's backs were turned. Getting stuff would be dead easy; what worried her was who these leaders were going to be. If she wasn't one of them – and she knew she wasn't one of the oldest there – she was going to be dead choosy about who gave orders to her.

And here came one of the possibles – rushing in with his church cassock over his arm: Jimmy Riley, straight from mass with Father Wearden at St Patrick's. She sat up as he slid into the row behind her, leaning over.

'Good morning to you, Jose.'

She turned and smiled and he winked, which pleased her: on account of Topper, of course. A wink like that meant he might let her have a ride later; which is why she went to the stables, wasn't it?

'We'll get what stuff we want,' Len was going on. 'An' if you don't know how, you're not much good to me.'

Josie stared up at her brother on the stage. He'd always been one for taking charge of things, the sort who'd be a stevedore by Christmas; but she'd never seen him taking charge like this. She sat there proud of that top dog up there.

'Now we ain't goin' off at half-cock. If Jerry comes over tonight, you get down Wilson's Wharf, all of you, and keep yourselves near the door with anything you've got hold of, but don't make no show of it. Wheel-barrers an' buckets of water, keep 'em round the corner in the alley, but stuff hammers down your trousers an' spanners up your jumpers. I'll be on the roof, bomb spotter, an' when I see Jerry drop something we can tackle I'll shout down. Then the leaders'll pick their men to go out. But tonight we play it as it comes, till we get organised. In a minute I'll tell you who these leaders are, then tomorrow they'll choose their proper crews and get the rest of their gear together. Right?'

*Right!* Already the boys were looking along the rows to see which kids these leaders might be, the men who'd be picking the crews. The place went quiet, everyone listening for the names.

Len looked up from his piece of paper. 'Right. These are them, an' I ain't having no arguments. It's what I say, 'cos I know about this – ' he levelled his iron bar at them – 'or you can do what you want out of some other shelter…'

Everyone's head was up; no Globe audience had ever sat so quiet.

'Me, I'm leading one team an' we'll pick different spotters for up on the roof on different nights; then it's gonna be...' There was a long pause while Len turned his piece of paper the right way up. 'Ray Gull, Dougie Raynor, Bert Brewer, an' one more, who I can't tell you till later.'

Ray, Dougie and Bert all sat there looking pleased with themselves. Ray smiled, Dougie waved, and Bert gave a short sharp nod.

'Why can't you tell us the other one?' Any one of the rest of them could be this last leader. 'Don't you know?'

'I know all right. But it's got to be kept quiet till tonight.'

Josie made a noise, a sudden sucking in of her breath which she had to turn into a cough. *Was it her?* Len knew she was lively, had run her Hermits gang to be the best around, could see off any idiot in Hermitage Quays. Was she his secret choice – only he wanted to check with her first?

'Come off it, Len. Why can't you tell us now, if you know?' Tony Milner was getting bolder.

'Because...'

'That ain't no answer. OK, tell us the "because", then. Leave out the name but tell us why you can't say it, you gotta give us that.'

Len put his piece of paper away, looked as if he was going to twist his iron bar round Milner's neck. What was he going to do? Generals had to be strong, but they had to know when to give a bit. So what would he say if it was her?

'All right, I'll tell you. It's because there's something about him his dad don't know yet. I saw him 's'morning, bit of a surprise all round, an' he's up for it, gonna be 'specially useful. An' that's all I'm saying till later on.'

Josie swore under her breath. Then it wasn't her. With Len being her brother, she'd really thought she was in with a chance; and she'd already got it in her head where half her gear was coming from. She stood up. 'Oi!'

For the first time Len seemed to notice her. 'An' you, Josie Turner – you can go home straight off.'

*Eh? What was he on about?* 'Go home?'

'Yes. Go home. Because we ain't having girls. Not leaders, an' not crew.'

*'What?'*

'You heard.'

Josie marched down the aisle, shouting up at him. 'You can't say girls can't join, Len Turner. You can't say girls like me can't be as good as any of this lot at squirting hoses an' getting old ladies down ladders…'

'I can say, an' I do say!'

'What about the fire brigade? They've got a girl riding a Matchless a bit tastier than you on your rusty ol' push-bike!'

One or two brave souls laughed.

'Shut up, Josie! There's no argy-bargy about it. Girls are out. And any young 'uns, too, for that matter. Aren't they?' He looked down at the rows of boys in front of him. And everyone cheered.

'You wait, Len Turner!' Josie was smouldering. 'I'll show you what girls can do! And young 'uns.' She stomped back to the entrance, pulled back the curtain and went out into the smoky air, any thoughts of seeing Goldie gone from her head.

And she meant what she'd said. Her dad had taught her how to box, Ivy had taught her how to stand up to stroppy neighbours, and no one in Hermitage Quays would ever want to fight her. She'd run the best gang going, and as soon as she looked old enough in a bit of lipstick and powder she was going to lie about her age and be a messenger on a Matchless. Len looked all in charge up there, but at home she was every bit as grown up as him, she knew all his secrets, sisters do. So it was two fingers in a 'V' to Len Turner and his kids' fire brigade. Anything he could do, she could, too!

Warden Bill Bailey had had only two hours' sleep before going out again on his duties. Now he came back to his house on the corner of Watts Place and Raymond Street. He let himself into the hallway, squeezed past his bicycle, and went through to the kitchen. And he stopped.

'Ye gods!'

Getting up from his seat at the kitchen table was his boy, Sonny.

'What the deuce are you doing here?'

Sonny looked nervous around the mouth, but there was defiance in his eyes. He was going on fifteen, and could have been doing a man's work in the docks by now. He shot a look across at his mother who was standing in the kitchen doorway, the homely smell of her Sunday roast mingling with the conflict in the air.

'I've come home.'

The man hadn't yet taken off his ARP helmet and dungarees. He stood there looking like a police officer about to make an arrest. 'I can see that. The question is, why? You been badly treated by the Bradshaws? You're not expelled from school, are you?' Sonny had been evacuated to Norfolk a year before with the boys' grammar school.

'Tons of the kids have come back. It's boring, school holidays with nothing to do, and now we're not starting back till we've got the harvest in. Slave labour, that's what it is.'

'No, *crucial* labour's what it is. You ought to see the docks. We lost half our imports last night. We need our harvest.' Bill Bailey stretched his body angrily until his belt creaked. 'You're going back, Monday. You didn't get a scholarship for nothing. We took a packet yesterday and we'll take another one today, you mark my words. An' you're going back where it's safe.'

Sonny gave his father a long stare before drumming his fingers on the table. He didn't argue, but his eyes said what he intended. 'Anyhow, it's good to see Mum. And you. And have a proper East End dinner.' He sniffed, like a Bisto kid. 'I saw Len Turner as I came from the train. He told me about stuff—'

'That one! Cheeky little tyke. He's trouble, you don't want too much to do with him.' Bill Bailey frowned. 'How'd you afford a train, anyhow?'

Sonny shrugged. 'Somehow.' But like a polite and obedient son he got up, went to the kitchen drawer and started laying the table for Sunday dinner – at the same time digging out his old sheath knife. He slipped it behind his belt on the inside of his trousers. 'What've we got, Mum?'

'Rabbit.'

'Not a proper joint, then?'

'You'll be lucky!' Bill Bailey was out of his dungarees and washing his hands at the kitchen sink. 'Beat old Hitler and we can all look forward to roast beef.'

'That's it.' Sonny straightened a fork on the table. 'Do our bit and beat old Hitler. That's the way.'

'So you get back and help with that harvest.'

'Oh, I'll definitely help.' But Sonny didn't say how; and at the first chance he got he took the sheath knife up to his bedroom and hid it under his mattress, on the bed that his mother had kept made up for him.

Josie was trying to get Len out of her system by grooming Topper. It helped, working hard on his flanks with a currycomb. This grey was special; most of the other horses in the stables were draughts, kept on while petrol was tight to pull carts to the railway. But Wilson's Wharf specialised in tea, and once a week Topper took deliveries of Lipton's to the smart West End shops: Harrods, Selfridges and Fortnum's. And off duty he was a good ride for Jimmy Riley, who was a natural of an Irish horseman, always with a chancy look in his eyes as he jumped him over park benches and across flowerbeds.

Rub, rub, rub, round in circles, watching Topper's hide shivering under the comb. 'He won't let me in 'cos I'm not a boy. So stuff his kids' fire brigade. Eh? Jimmy?'

'Oh, I'll be up for it meself, when Elijah an' Ellie are looking to the horses. We did all right with the fire, didn't we?'

They had; but the smell of doused burning was still strong, and Jimmy sounded tired. She knew he'd been up all night calming the horses, nuzzling them, putting cotton wool in their ears. He'd shown her where he'd been kicked and had his toes trodden on; and she wished Ivy had let her come round last night. It would have been good to be part of it.

'Anyhow, I'm as strong as any boy, an' I'm leaving school at Christmas, so what's Len's gripe?'

Jimmy turned his head at her under his arm, like a bird beneath its wing. 'Could be you're too bonny a lass to get the grime on your face.'

*What was that?* Bonny meant beautiful, he'd once said it about a poster of Maureen O'Hara. She rubbed harder with the curry. 'Shut up, Jimmy Riley. Keep your blarney to yourself!' She knew she'd gone red, and she didn't like going red.

'So, what are you going to do about brother Len? Take it quietly, like?' Jimmy went to fetch fresh feed.

'Oh, I'm going to do something, all right. But I'm not telling you – you'll go blabbing it when you see him.'

'I will not.' Jimmy moved on to a horse in another stall, further away. He didn't seem bothered, anyhow. 'When you've finished with the curry, get on with the dandy-brush – short strokes, front to back.'

'I know!' She was still red from what Jimmy had said. Being pretty or not had never much come into things. But she couldn't deny he'd given her a buzz.

She shook her head and thought of something else. When she'd finished here she'd go round to all the

Hermits' houses to tell them what she was up to, a plan that was coming together in her head. And then Len could see what she was made of – and it definitely wasn't being bonny, or sugar and spice and all things nice. No way.

Still…Jimmy putting her up with Maureen O'Hara… that could make anyone go red, couldn't it?

The bombers came over again. That night the shelter was crowded with a hundred people. Some hadn't waited for the siren to sound, they'd gone down early to get themselves the best places, commandeering seats to put their cushions on and taking a foot or so of space for their bits and pieces – a puppy, a canary in a cage, a family vase, handbags and gas masks. Micky had brought in more chairs, made a First Aid corner for a Red Cross woman, hung mothballs in the lavatory area, found more mugs, and rigged up a camping-gas ring for making tea. But in all the talk the changes were hardly noticed. Everyone had a horror story to tell – like the rumour going around that a bomb had hit Columbia Road shelter last night, killing more than forty people.

Micky tried to squash wild talk but he was busy and that made it easy for Len's brigade to start operating. His lads were told to keep near the doorway away from mothers, aunts and sisters, and pretend to play cards and penny-up-the-wall, while Dougie, Ray and Bert were to take turns to stand outside and listen for his shouts coming down.

'Oi! Mind that blackout!' That was Micky's other main concern.

The raiders were hitting the East End hard. The sounds of the bombing rang around the shelter and shock waves shook its floor again. Outside, the noise was intense – German planes droning over and sometimes swooping and diving to get out of the searchlights, with ground ack-ack firing up at them, RAF guns rattling, ships' sirens wailing, police whistles blowing – and bombs crunching down on buildings, streets, and ships in the docks. The air was thick with smoke and oil, with burning hemp, spirits and wood stacks mingling with ash, feathers, tattered bits of sheet and burning wallpaper fluttering up from people's homes.

Considering this was its first night Len's system worked well. He was up on the roof in a sailor's steel helmet shouting down where incendiaries were landing.

'Sisal Street – shed on fire.'

Dougie ran back inside, slapped four boys round the head and ran up the steps and out again. The four boys dropped their cards and galloped after him.

Soon after it was Ray's turn. 'Back of Billy's Diner, stack of crates blazing up the wall.' The same again, with four more boys chasing out to their equipment in the alley.

Josie kept herself near the doorway. Tonight she was dressed for a cold night below ground in slacks, jumper, and headscarf. Ivy was dressed the same with a touch of fur, but sitting as far away from the smell of the lavatory as she could get. Josie chose her moment and told her she was going to play cards with the boys – 'For matchsticks, not money.' She wasn't, though, she wanted to keep a close eye on Len's crews – and when she first got over there she suddenly found out who that other leader was: and what a surprise! Sonny Bailey the warden's boy, someone she'd not seen around for a year. There he was, lounging at the top of the stairs as if he was outside the Globe waiting for a mate, his hair glossy with Brylcreem and with that same old cocky look on his face. But no surprise, really. Sonny Bailey was boxing champion of the district, who'd been going to meet Len in the final of the Metropolitan Youth Cup before evacuation called it off. Len and Sonny could stand eye to eye with one another, different sorts, but both handy, and both ready to punch hard till the final bell.

Now suddenly it was Sonny's turn, taking his orders from Len on the roof. He ran back inside. 'You, you and you.' He poked three boys. 'Behind Johnson's dairy! Two fire bombs! Chop-chop, look lively!' He sounded like a chip off the old Bailey block.

Josie watched his crew go running out, and she felt useless. Hitler was giving London another good pasting – worse than the night before – and in no time the boys in the doorway were thinned out to nothing, so there would definitely have been fires to fight for some other teams.

'Wait till tomorrow,' she told Shirley. 'If it's like tonight they'll be blooming pleased there's another lot to go out.

'Who's that, Jose?'

'Us! The Hermits!'

'Us?'

'Yeah! The Hermits!'

'The Hermits!' Shirley repeated it – like an oath she was taking. They'd done that sort of thing before, but now in the danger of the raid it sounded very grown-up, and deadly, deadly serious.

The Germans had come back big time – and, the same as everyone else in the shelter, Josie reckoned they were in this for a hell of a long stretch.

# 6

Josie went to the stables to see Goldie. Lou had cleaned her up, washed out her clothes, and taken her back to Elijah's flat until her mother came out of the infirmary – if that ever happened.

'You're all right, then? Not a ghost like the kids thought? You got blown over by the bomb?'

'Don't know, Jose – I was running meself home and the next thing I was sitting in Miss Lou's flat, all dirty an' white… But I don't remember nothing in the middle.'

'Amnesia, child. That's the word for it.' Elijah looked tired; he'd got the stables to run, his daughter to fret over, and Goldie to care for. Josie thought if either of the two Bostons looked like a ghost it was him.

She'd seen the Monday clear-up going on, heard a few people hoping the bombing had been a weekend thing; but the wireless said to be ready for the raiders coming back tonight, and she reckoned it was right. Last night had definitely had the feel to it of a war to the death.

Len had gone off early to his work at St Katharine Dock, not a word about his fire brigade in front of Ivy, and he'd shut Josie up when she'd started talking about stirrup pumps – but from the way he'd cleared a space in the shed she knew he was coming home later with a tool or two down his shirt, ready for the Germans coming back.

She wanted to tell Goldie what was going on. She needed everyone she could get for the Hermits' Fire Brigade: even a young 'un like Goldie could shovel sand, or if she couldn't get out she could help find the stuff they needed.

The stable was busy, the horses in and out pulling carts from the Western Dock or to the station, Prince back from an early shift, and Jimmy in the street hitching Holly and Tess to a wagon. She needed Goldie where she could talk privately away from Ellie the stable lass.

'Come on, Gold. Let's give old Prince a drink.'

'He's just had a drink.'

Josie gave her a look. 'He's puckering up, still looks thirsty to me.' She pulled Goldie away, put the bucket in front of Prince, who tossed his mane and ignored it. 'Listen, Gold…' Heads down, both stroking Prince on his further side, she told the girl how her fire brigade was going to work. 'See, it's gonna be us, doin' the same as Len and his lot, putting out fires with sand and water. There'll be tons of places to go, there was last night…'

Goldie listened. 'I'll come if I can. I'll definitely be down the shelter, but Grampy's gonna keep putting his head in to see I'm OK.' She shivered. 'Better than Miss Lou's place; it shook like wobble-jelly last night.'

'Well, I'll be down there, an' as many Hermits as poss.

An' try an' bring one of these.' Josie casually kicked the water bucket. 'We need our own stuff.'

'Yeah, OK.' Goldie frowned. 'So, like, we're the Hermits…what does Len's men call their-selves?'

Josie blew out her cheeks. 'Dunno.' Len wouldn't talk about it because he always seemed scared of starting a row.

'"The Dead End Kids".'

'What?'

The voice had come from the other side of Prince. It was Jimmy's. 'Your man's calling it the "The Dead End Kids".'

'How d'you know that?'

'I'm in it, aren't I, when I can. When Elijah's back from the infirmary I'm in for the craic. And Len's told me about it.'

Josie swore. Len's name for his fire brigade was terrific – much better than 'The Hermits'. He'd got it from the kids in the gangster films – their poster was in the Hole. Funny boy film stars, all mouth and trousers: Tommy, Angel, Milty, Spit and Dippy, they put two fingers up at the police and people like Warden Bailey, kids winning over the grown-ups.

She'd got to do something about this. And quick. 'Forgot to tell you, Gold. I've changed our name.' She stood up straight, the leader, but not knowing what she was going to say until it came out. 'We're gonna be the "East Side Gang"' – which was a stroke, her suddenly coming up with another famous film name. 'How about that?'

'Smashing.'

'Ah-ha.' Jimmy laughed. 'So now there'll be two jolly wars going on. The Germans against the British, and the Dead End Kids against the East Side Gang…'

Josie stared him in the face, this other Jimmy – the rival. 'You bet! An' let the best side win…'

'Oh, that'll happen sure enough. That's the way it's supposed to, isn't it – leastways in the flicks I've seen…'

One of her problems was getting the gang out of the shelter to fight fires. Mums and aunties weren't going to say, 'Off you go, just try and dodge the bombs.' But the shelter was big, and going by what she'd seen the last two nights none of the grown-ups wanted kids under their feet for hour after hour – like, a lot of chat wasn't for children to hear, it was grown-up stuff told with their hands over their mouths. And Ivy hadn't kicked up when she'd drifted away, provided she'd showed herself from time to time. But the younger kids would have to give their people the slip, too, and some nights they wouldn't all make it. Then she wouldn't have enough; so she'd got to get some others for cover. Well, she'd work on that, but it would all sort itself out somehow.

For when it did, the East Side Gang also needed

wheels. Buckets of water, tins of sand and a stirrup pump couldn't be lugged around in their hands, not when they were running to a fire. But wheelbarrows weren't much use, Len's lot had found that out. When the handles were picked up the bucket was on a slope and water went slopping all over everything. So Josie's favourite would be a box-cart like the soapbox on wheels her dad had made for her. But Len had bagged it, and it would take a war of its own to get it off him. There were other wheels about, though. When kids wanted wheels for box-carts they kept their eyes on every pram and pushchair around, anything that might be going begging when a toddler got too big. Begging, borrowing, or stealing…

She walked up and down the streets with wheels in her head. She tried to keep her eyes shut to the terrible damage from the night before, wouldn't stop to talk to anyone, and didn't let herself get drawn to a cordoned-off corner where Civil Defence were still digging people out from a smoking heap of a house. She was a leader on a mission.

It took her to where a few shops were open.

'*Business as Usual*';

'*Hitler – show your coupons*';

'*Yes, we have no bananas*'.

People were queuing – mostly women, and with women there were kids: toddlers and babies in pushchairs and prams. Sure enough, outside Coopers' the greengrocer's there was a woman with a pram she couldn't get in through the door. Josie sidled up to it; but instead of a sleeping baby it was a sharp-eyed girl sitting up; and, anyway, what would she have done with a baby? And when she looked at the wheels they had spindly spokes; they wouldn't be much good for bumping over cobbles.

She went on – and outside the Port of London offices she saw just what she wanted. Dockers' wives were lining up for handouts, and one woman in the queue had a canvas pushchair with a good set of wheels. It was soppy Donny Duncan sitting in it sucking a dummy – and, well, Josie wouldn't be up to much if she couldn't get one over on him. She hovered, pretended to do up her sandals and looked under the seat – and saw what she'd hoped for: the pushchair had four wing nuts holding the seat to the chassis. Unscrew them, and – t'riffic! – the wheels were hers. She went around the corner for a think. She knew these docks offices, and the good thing for her was that while the docks business was done on the ground floor, the housing stuff and the handouts were done upstairs: she knew, she'd been here often enough. This meant that Donny's mum was going to have to leave the pushchair down below while she queued on the stairs. But the question was, would she leave Donny in it, or would she take him up with her? Well, things looked hopeful. The queue was moving so slowly, and Donny was such a big cry-baby, he'd kick off pretty quickly if he was left down there on his own. Or she could make him cry to get him picked up. The thing was not to show herself till she made her move: she didn't want people remembering Josie Turner hanging around that pushchair.

She joined onto the back of the queue, tucked herself in like another bombed-out sad case, and shuffled forward with the rest, keeping her head down. Lots of older daughters did errands like this, especially with a war on. She was around the corner from the front, well away from Donny and his mum who'd soon be going inside the building – so no one could finger her as being anywhere near the pushchair just yet. She moved on slowly, kept patient, listened to everyone, all too full of their troubles to bother speaking to her. She bided her time, leant on the wall, moved on a bit, did some more leaning, then just before shuffling round the corner, she quietly slipped out of the queue and walked to the front, arms folded across her chest as if she was on her way to have a stroppy word with someone.

Donny and his mother weren't outside, nor was the pushchair. Well, that made sense. An empty pushchair on the pavement would be a right temptation for some tea-leaf or other.

''Scuse. 'Scuse me. Want a word with my mum.' Still making no fuss, she squeezed past a woman in the doorway and went into the hallway.

And there was Donny's pushchair, over in a corner by the Employment Office, with Mrs Duncan a couple of steps up the stairs telling Donny he was too big to be carried.

She went outside, waited a while, and came in again, timed it just right for when Mrs Duncan was getting near the handout door. Quickly, but for all the world as if she'd been sent to fetch it, she took hold of the pushchair, wheeled it to the door and went out again, not stopping for anything. Round one corner and then another and she wasn't far from where Civil Defence were still digging, so no one took any notice of her. She stopped, unscrewed the wing nuts, threw the canvas seat over the remains of a wall, and went off with the chassis – which was on four good wheels. She'd get Arthur to make a wooden body to go on top of it and they'd paint 'East Side Gang' on the side. She smiled. 'Right, Len Turner! – my lot's in business!'

She scooted on the chassis towards the barge, hid it, and walked back past the PLA building where Mrs Duncan was carrying Donny home. And she only just resisted the temptation to give the pair of them a little wave.

Job done.

As she knew it would, the siren went again that night.

She and Ivy ran to the shelter as the distant sound of droning grew in the sky.

'Blighters! Won't leave it, will they?'

Len hadn't been at home, and when they reached the shelter she saw why. His boys had claimed one of the small arched alcoves in the shelter and put up a sign: 'DEAD END KIDS' DEPARTMENT" – a message to everyone that they were a proper in-the-open outfit. On the alcove shelves were gas masks, dockers' leather gloves, bottles of lemonade and a row of different torch batteries. And on a wide shelf Sonny Bailey was lying back with a folded blanket under his head. That's what Len had been up to.

Now she wanted her own alcove with their own sign up, 'EAST SIDE GANG HQ'. Ivy sat nowhere over here, and if Micky had let one lot have a sign he couldn't say no to the other. But she was short of members and she didn't have the clout. Len's was a going fire brigade, while without more people hers was no more than a might-happen.

She'd already started by trying to enlist Jimmy at the stables; but he wouldn't have it, the same old story.

'Not a chance, I don't take no orders from a girl, not even Josie Turner…'

She shouldn't have bothered: with his dad in the army Jimmy was the man of the house, helped his mum put food on the table for the kids. Tall, soft voice, a bit of a will-o'-the-wisp, he was gentler than most Hermitage Quays lads, which came out when he talked to his horses, but between her and him she knew who'd always have the last word. He would. And, to be honest, she'd let him, the blue-eyed boy. But that didn't help the East Side Gang.

The bombers started giving the docks another pounding, and it needed fingers in the ears to shut out the sounds of fire engines and ambulances and heavy demolition. Getting away from Ivy – 'Gonna see if the First Aid lady wants any bandages rolled up' – Josie stood in the doorway, listening to Len up on the roof, shouting down where his next crew had to go. Suddenly it was Dougie Raynor's lot – and blow her if it wasn't Jimmy Riley going out with them. She hadn't seen him come in.

He waved back to her. 'Here we go, then.'

'Yeah.' Josie wished it was her with the East Side Gang, but that would be tomorrow, when Arthur had finished making their box-cart and she'd got more crew. Meanwhile, she crossed her fingers for Jimmy Riley, out under the bombs on a call.

Dougie Raynor and his men ran their pram to Platt Street, where a fire was getting a hold in the roof-space. Downstairs was empty but the street-door gave quickly with a few whacks from an axe – where they were met by smoke coming rolling down the stairs. But after the night before they knew what to do. They pulled scarves and neckerchiefs up over their mouths and with buckets, sand and the stirrup pump they climbed to the first floor flat.

Old Mr and Mrs Rosenberg were sloshing pans of water at the curtains and skirting boards.

'Faster. Gelda, faster!'

But the problem was the wooden laths up behind the ceiling plaster, burning through and threatening to drop fire around their heads.

'Shut the ruddy door!' Dougie – a docker like Len – was a good leader, too. 'Get that other bucket filled!' He uncoiled the hose of the stirrup pump, and as Jimmy ran through to the kitchen he started pumping and aiming.

But the Rosenbergs hadn't heard about the Dead End Kids. 'Who are you? You're *kinder*, not firemen!'

'Oh, yes we are! You leave it to us – an' get yourselves down the shelter.'

'Firemen are firemen. You're—'

'Firemen! What's this – water. What's this – a hose. What else d'you want, a slide down our pole?'

'*Feh!* I'm not leaving this place, I tell you!'

Jimmy ran in from the kitchen with a full bucket.

'Go on, out you get!' Dougie pointed the Rosenbergs towards the door. 'Willy, get 'em out an' down the shelter. We'll sort this.'

But Isaac Rosenberg was standing firm. 'I come from Germany to get away from Hitler, I leave my home there, my business.' He coughed in the thickening smoke, fighting for more breath. 'I don't leave this place, Adolf Hitler doesn't tell Isaac Rosenberg...what he should do...'

'Come!' Gelda Rosenberg pulled at his arm. 'For two hours, three. What's to steal? You want to die from your chest? Or I should die?' She coughed, too.

'Go on, Pop! We won't be long.' Dougie was winning, bent over and keeping his men low where the breathing was better; the fire was nearly out, but the smoke was thick and everyone was coughing. 'You ain't got the chest for this. Give us the key, we'll finish off. We'll lock up an' bring it down the shelter.'

Isaac Rosenberg still hesitated. His wife went to the sideboard, took a photograph of a child from a drawer. 'I go. You stay and choke on your pride.'

The final hosing went on, the smoke getting worse. Isaac sighed, and lifted his black hat from the back of the door; which was the signal for his wife to take a key from a cup on the sideboard and give it to Jimmy. 'Turn twice,' she said. 'Once for the door, twice for burglars.' She led Isaac out, both ushered down the stairs by Willy, to be followed soon after by the rest.

'Come on, Mrs Rosenberg, step lively.' And, overtaking the elderly couple, Jimmy made a little geeing-up sound in his throat, as if he was working Topper…

It was a busy night for the Dead End Kids. As well as the high explosives, incendiary bombs were dropping all over Hermitage Quays. Josie was jealous and frustrated as she saw Jimmy in the shelter, one minute giving a key to old Mr Rosenberg, and running out the next to a call-out with Dougie. Lucky devil! The same with the other crews – they were all go, and she was all stop.

The All Clear sounded just before dawn and she started thinking about the things she'd got to get done later that day.

'See you, Jose!' Jimmy waved goodbye and ran off out of the shelter, beating most of the old 'uns to the door. He was rushing to the stables to check his horses, she reckoned, and she wanted to go there with him – to make sure Topper was all right. But Ivy came round the corner and wouldn't hear of it. So she walked home with her like an obedient daughter, feeling nothing like one inside.

And she wouldn't have found him at the stables if she had gone.

Slinking along by the river Jimmy made his way back to the Rosenbergs' building, where the street door was still smashed in – and the door to their flat the way he'd left it: pulled to, but unlocked. He slipped inside. The light was coming up in the sky, another fine day, and the way could be seen into the kitchen. An interrupted meal was on the kitchen table covered by a cloth, two places. In the middle was a plate of cold cuts, a saucer of margarine, and half a loaf of dark, braided bread. Turning to the kitchen drawer, Jimmy rummaged around, found a sisal bag, and quickly cleared the meal into it. He opened a cupboard where there were two eggs on a plate, a jar of calves'-foot jelly, and a tin of baked beans. He wrapped the eggs in torn sheets of newspaper and put them into the bag with the rest. The light through the kitchen window was getting stronger, and voices could be heard in the street. Quickly, he tipped over the kitchen table and threw a pan of water onto the floor, as if everything had happened in the emergency of filling the buckets. He doubled back through the living room, seeing old Mr Rosenberg's steel watch hanging on the dresser, which he ignored, and opening the door he listened hard before going on careful feet down the stairs to check the street through the smashed woodwork.

And within fifteen minutes he was at home, putting breakfast food on the table for his family in the morning.

'Get that fodder in your bellies,' he said quietly.

# 7

'He's a good boy, Father.' Eileen Riley was sweeping up strips of lead and stained glass from the nave of St Patrick's Church, saving the larger pieces in separate buckets. 'He looks to our needs.'

'And to mine. He's my strength when I need it.' The frail, elderly priest looked as if strength was a long-lost part of his make-up. 'But I'm chasing your case, be assured.'

Money from Private Riley was slow coming through, an army disgrace according to the priest.

'And you're looking sprightly yourself this morning.'

'I had a decent breakfast today, Father. Someone gave Jimmy a few bits an' pieces.'

'Very kind of them. And the little ones?'

'Don't they love scrambled eggs? Maureen next door's looking after them.'

'Then I shan't keep you late. Tell Jimmy to come round when he's done with his horses and he can help board up that window.'

Eileen Riley looked at the high altar, where the priest was brushing off plaster. 'Are you not putting that away, Father?' She pointed to the crucifix in the centre of the altar, left there from early-morning mass. 'We wouldn't want our Lord more injured than he was at Calgary.

And it must be worth a few shillings…'

'It's symbolic.' The priest stroked his hand down it. 'Our protection. He's always to be here, witness, for all the world to see.'

'You know what's best in the faith, Father.' Eileen Riley made the sign of the cross but finished by patting her tight belly. 'And you know our earthly needs.'

'I'm doing my best, Eileen, doing my best.'

Eileen Riley bent to her task, concentrating on the broken glass. 'I know you are, Father, you're a good man.'

Station Officer Ralph Wiltshire had unfastened his collar and was walking towards the headteacher's office carrying a doughnut and a cup of tea. It was mid-morning. Out in the playground fire appliances were being cleaned and serviced while exhausted off-watch firemen slept in the classrooms on either side of the school hall. As SO Wiltshire passed the door marked 'Mrs Nunn, Junior 4', he stood for a moment, put his tea and doughnut behind his back, and nodded his head, a curt bow of respect. Four beds were empty in there this morning: those of AFS volunteers who hadn't come back from the East India Dock, killed by a direct hit on an oil tank: men he'd trained pre-war and whose wives and kids he knew like family.

In the office Joyce Fleming handed him a memo pad

with a message from Division. He sat, dunked his doughnut – 'tea and buns', fire crew comforts – blowing out his cheeks as he read the memo. He wiped sugar off the paper. 'You read this?'

'I wrote it out, sir.'

'Sunday night. Two hundred and fifty of the blighters up there, dropped don't know how many hundred tons of high explosive and enough incendiaries to start the second Fire of London… I told 'em we were overwhelmed.'

'But read the last bit.'

'A thousand pumps deployed in the Surrey Docks alone, so God knows what numbers were like over this side of the river…'

'And the very last bit,' she prompted.

He blew out his cheeks again. 'About time. Appliances are coming down from Northampton, Lincoln, all over. As long as we get some here.' He coughed on a bit of doughnut. 'Last night I was juggling pumps like a circus turn, now two of them are wreckage.' He coughed again, couldn't clear the blockage. 'Lord, I don't know what they put in these doughnuts.'

'TNT, from the sounds of it.' But Joyce knew it wasn't the doughnut choking him; it was his boys. His dead boys.

Josie and the East Side Gang were almost in business,

using the Hermit Hole as their base. Arthur had made the box-cart, a yard and a half long from front wheels to back with rope steering; Shirley had brought a sterilising bucket from her dad's shed, being kept until he came home from the war and opened up his barber's shop again; and from his mother's café Eddie Rossi had brought a catering flour drum filled with sand. Arthur had filched a blunt chopper from under a tarpaulin in his aunt's back yard; and Josie had strolled across to Jubilee House and come away with the star prize: one of two stirrup pumps from the entrance hall right outside Charlie Drew's flat.

But she needed more than this. She needed more people. Arthur was solid, he'd always take a whack from 'Uncle Jack' if it was for the gang, but he wouldn't always get out from under. Eddie, who sometimes helped in the café, went around the shelter with Micky's cups of tea and bits and pieces his mama dished out to be popular, so he could be out of her sight and off on a raid, but she was too fond of holding his hand for comfort. Mrs Farmer – who was in the WVS and had driven their tea van two nights running – brought Shirley to the shelter and had given her to a neighbour and gone off, so with a bit of cunning Shirley could be free. As for Josie herself, Ivy said she was going to do a bit of singing around the shelters some nights, which was good news. Auntie Varley was a regular sitter for Ivy's late pub nights if Len wasn't home. She came in from next door, or Josie went in there. But the old lady liked a little drop of 'medicine' so her eyes would soon start to droop, and when her mouth dropped open she'd be good for an hour at least. So if Ivy did go out singing it would be even easier getting away. Everyone knew everyone in Hermitage Quays, and they all knew everyone's kids. There seemed to be more 'aunties' around than there were dockers and they'd usually 'keep an eye' for a mother, especially with soldiers and men off ships around. But their eyes weren't always as sharp and their concentration not as good, so they often let kids do things their mothers would throw a fit at.

All of which meant that running a skeleton crew was possible, but the four of them definitely wouldn't be enough.

With the stirrup pump safely hidden in the Hole, Josie left the others and went back to Charlie Drew's flat. His mother came to the door looking anxious. Any knock could be serious in wartime.

'Yes?'

'Please can Charlie come out to play, Mrs Drew?'

The woman frowned, looked Josie up and down. 'What's all this about?' She looked past Josie to see what trick she was up to. 'Big girl like you, ought to be out to work – not chucking mud at him Saturday.'

'Bit of fun with the young'uns, that was all.'

'Bit of fun? I'm still getting the Creek out of his underpants.'

'Don' matter, then. Just wondered.' She turned to go. But she'd spoken especially loud and Charlie had heard her. He came to the door, and going by the crumpled comic in his hand and the state of his hair he had to be bored stiff.

'Turner! What you want?' He scowled at her.

What to say, in front of his mum? 'We're 'aving a game of Matchsticks Rummy over the barge. Two packs of new cards from…where my mum sings…could do with another player, Arthur's goin' home in a minute.'

Mrs Drew's neck bent a fraction towards Charlie as if a game of cards sounded like a nice clean thing to be doing for a couple of hours – and Josie had the chance to give Charlie a wink. 'Just, if you like.' She moved away, take-it-or-leave-it, the old dodge.

Charlie took it. 'I might come over, then.'

'Up to you.'

She went; but she'd hooked him, and it wasn't five minutes before he was down in the Hole with the Hermits – where there weren't any playing cards, old or new. But he didn't look surprised by that. What kids said to people's mums and what they did were two different things.

'You ever heard of the Dead End Kids?'

'The film lot, or your Len's fire brigade?'

'You in it, in one of his crews?' She knew he wasn't.

'Nah. We're not over your shelter, are we? We got the basement here.'

Ah. She hadn't thought of that. 'But if you was good enough to be in it, could you get over to ours in the raids? Could you be that sharp, dodging your mum?'

With her putting it like that, Charlie's face said it didn't need thinking about. 'Most times. Basement's got all different parts. We got places where we muck about on our own. Don't see her some nights from the siren to the All Clear.'

'An' you can get out?'

'Easy.'

'But would you want to?' She put on a look as if she was having second thoughts. 'Would you be up to nicking a tin hat an' being a fireman some nights?'

'You jokin'?' But he scowled. 'What you on about? Len wouldn't 'ave me. They reckon 'e's got his men, an' his reserves...'

She leaned towards him. Arthur did, too, from the other side. 'I could use you, though. 'Cos I've got my own fire brigade, the East Side Gang, an' right now I'm getting an ace crew together. An' it happens I've got a few spare places for kids who don't wet their knickers when a firework goes off.'

'You?'

'*Me!*'

Charlie started scowling again.

She turned her head away. 'Right, Arf, I said I'd ask him. He's not up for it, so we'll get over the bridge and 'ave a word with the Bus Depot Boys. They've got some proper tough numbers there.'

'Hang on a minute, Turner.'

She hung on.

'I'll give it a go, if I can bring a couple of my gang.'

'Will you? How long after the siren can you be down our shelter?'

'Twenny minutes? P'raps ten.'

She looked at Arthur as if the two of them were making a decision. But there was no decision to make. If Charlie Drew and a couple more were in, the East Side Gang could get going. 'Make it a quarter of an hour, top whack?'

'Yeah, all right.'

'An' only your three best men? Reckon you could?'

'I reckon.'

'We need equipment an' all. Got any crowbars an' shovels – an' p'raps a stirrup pump…?'

Eddie had a coughing fit.

Charlie thought about it. 'Prob'ly.'

'OK – but forget the last bit.' And for half an hour she, Charlie, and the others talked East Side Gang Fire Brigade, before Josie went home for her dinner, and Arthur stayed in the Hole and made sure the box-cart axles were oiled and ready. When they got their first call-out their wheels had to run a treat along the Hermitage streets.

During the day some of Len's Dead End Kids had been working on their alcove, while Micky was in and out trying to make the shelter better all the time, putting a few bunks in for disabled people and hanging curtains to give some sort of privacy. With a dead muscle and a limp from the Great War he seemed to relish his mission. Now he went into his own little cubbyhole, came out with a large cardboard box and took it to the alcove. 'Here, I got these for you.'

Sonny took it from him, opened it. Stacked inside like new bowler hats were six steel helmets.

'Tin hats!' Sonny pulled one out; then made a face. 'WVS' was painted on the front. 'Women's Voluntary Service?'

'They're surplus. Take 'em or leave 'em.'

'Oh, we'll take them. A drop of black paint and then we can chalk our names up front, whoever's wearing it…'

'Good luck to you. But chalk's a good idea, you can rub that out. Because one of you's gonna cop it one night, sure as eggs is eggs…'

'Be nice.' Ray Gull did a little dance.

'*Nice?* Copping it?'

'Eggs.' He started singing. *'I haven't had an egg since Easter, an' now it's half-past three, so, chick chick chick chick chicken, lay a little egg for me.'*

'That's the spirit. Make light of it – but Hitler don't intend to, just you remember that...'

# 8

The siren sounded at seven o'clock, earlier than usual.

'Damn blighters!' Ivy had just started making-up for a midweek turn in the Pirate cellar. 'Now they'll have to have me as I am.'

After his shift at the docks Len was out and about somewhere with his iron bar, but as the siren's wailing went on Ivy and Josie picked up their shelter things and hurried down Monks Street.

The regulars had already arrived with their thermos flasks, blankets, gas masks and cushions. Most families, though – home from work with a quick meal inside them – went to the shelter only when they had to. Josie always went dutifully with Ivy, carried what she was told to carry, and made sure to sit near her for a time and be a bit annoying. In a while she'd be allowed to drift off: fit in, then break out. Anyway, when a lull came Ivy would be off to the Pirate, and Auntie Varley would be in charge. Nice one.

As Ivy got into a hush-hush conversation about 'someone we all know' who was cheating on her husband with a bus conductor, Josie quietly slid away and met up with Eddie, Shirley, Charlie Drew and three of his Jubilees; she saw Arthur come in with his auntie and put his thumbs up: the East Side box-cart was parked in the alley, all set to go. He was going to tell his auntie it was for helping Micky lug stuff about, and the buckets were for the lavvy.

And over they came, the enemy, nearly half an hour of them in the first wave, pounding the docks and the City; with everyone's eardrums dulled by the bombing and the firing from ack-ack in the parks.

The Dead End Kids were already in the shelter doorway, Sonny Bailey at the top of the steps in a WVS steel helmet chalked with 'SB', listening for word coming down from Len up there fire-watching – although Sonny wasn't going to be first out. Word was, it was Bert Brewer's crew first, and then Ray Gulls', Sonny Bailey's and lastly Dougie Raynor's. But tonight the East Side Gang was ready, too, and Josie was determined it was going to be hers after that, even if any of the others came back. So she'd keep an eye out for Ivy leaving – be playing snap or something when she came through. Arthur had brought a small book of the gospels and told his aunt he wanted to read it somewhere quiet; and the others had used their own tricks to make it away from their minders. Len and the older kids could be all upfront about what they were doing but mostly being younger, the East End Gang had to be clever not to get sat on all night.

Including Josie. Ivy was coming through the shelter towards the steps, so in a flash she crouched down and pretended she'd just rolled a marble. 'Sugar! Missed.'

'See you later, Josie. You be good.'

'An' you be safe.'

'Do me best.' And Ivy went.

Josie gave her time to get clear and went up the steps to stand with Sonny, who was still listening for instructions.

She didn't know what Ivy thought about Len not being down the shelter. She had to know something was going on with him, she wasn't daft. But where Len was concerned Ivy seemed to know when to turn a blind eye.

The bombing was as bad as before. From the sounds of it there couldn't be a dock or a warehouse that wasn't taking a hit; but in the noise of the raid Len's voice came shouting down: he must have got hold of a megaphone.

'Baxter's Sacks! Fire bomb!'

Josie knew the sack factory in Ellis Street wouldn't be a top fire brigade priority, not up against the ships and the oil tanks and timber stacks; but it was in a tight corner of buildings, and there was all that sisal inside that could easily spread along a street. Bert Brewer gave his men the 'come on', and out they chased.

Josie called her gang in tighter. Some nights the raids had been along the river, or over the other side, but tonight it sounded like the Royal Docks were suffering, and that meant them. Len's shouts from the roof were going to come thick and fast.

So this was it. Nearly. In no time the East Side Gang

were going to be out on a call.

They stood ready, nervous feet, not-sure faces, Shirley wearing a WVS helmet she'd kept hidden in a bag, Arthur in a toy-shop tin hat, Eddie with a chin-strapped cooking pot lid, and Josie pulling out one of her dad's caps, padded with old stockings to make it fit.

'Looks like Gerry's Caff! Or next door. Not sure.'

Ray Gull and his crew were halfway out of the shelter, anyway, while Sonny Bailey had his head cocked, ready to go next.

''S'all right, Sonny – you ain't the only ones.' Josie was up behind him.

'Yeah, we're next.'

'Then us.'

'Who, *you*?' He had that usual cocky look on his face.

'Yes, us! The East Side Gang. You wanna make something of it?'

He looked just like his dad, a dead ringer. Bossy. Thought himself a cut above.

'Council rent office!' Len shouted.

'Let the place burn!' But Sonny was running off fast with his men.

Dougie Raynor moved his crew up the stairs. But he was a man short tonight. Jimmy Riley wasn't there, had to be at the stables still, calming his horses.

'You 'aven't got Jimmy.'

'I'll take Phil.' Dougie pulled Phil Jupp up a couple

of stairs, a large boy who started grinning like Fatty Arbuckle.

'No, you hang on for Jimmy. We'll do the next one.' Josie gave Phil a push back a couple of steps, elbowed Dougie aside and jostled her crew up the stairs; and just as she stuck her head outside Len shouted down again.

'Bus Depot Bridge! Fire! No AFS anywhere near!'

The wooden bridge. That was vital, it was the only way into the Western basin.

Already, Arthur was out and pulling the East Side box-cart from the alley along Wharf Road.

'Get a move on! If that goes up the fire brigade can't get to nothing!'

They pelted along as fast as Donny Duncan's pushchair wheels could turn, buckets clanging and water slopping – past King Henry's Wharf, the London River pub, the Captain Lowry Stairs, round the last bend – and there it was, the Bus Depot bridge ablaze, bright flames below and thick smoke hiding the tops of the warehouses.

'Bridge down flat, worse luck!' Eddie ran ahead and pointed at the horizontal burning planks. Flames were spreading fast across its middle. There were no buses on the other side, and no bus men about – there'd be no help from over there, then. Arthur pushed the stirrup pump into a bucket and started pumping, aiming a fierce jet at the flames. Josie uncoiled a length of rope from over Charlie Drew's shoulder and tied it to their second bucket, dropping it into the basin and pulling it up full.

They needed the stirrup pump to get to the far side of the fire, but closer in they were filling and chucking, filling and chucking. And after a while crackle became sizzle, and they knew they'd beaten the fire, which left a hole in the bridge but with room for wheels on either side of it.

'Oi! What are you kids doing here?' Warden Bailey had come running from somewhere.

'What's it look like we're doing?' Josie wasn't letting him have a go at her crew. Without them the whole bridge would have gone up in flames – which would have meant this side of Hermitage Quays being cut off. She drew breath to tell him his fortune, but she suddenly turned her head away as she heard a sound she knew. A Matchless was coming towards them, and on it was the AFS messenger she'd seen before, who was looking dead serious in her steel helmet as she parked up and ran onto the bridge, looking at the damage.

'You've done a good job here,' she told Warden Bailey. 'And lucky the planks run lengthwise, should be able to get our engines across.'

Josie turned to stare into Bailey's face. What was he going to say to that? Was he going to take a bow for putting out the fire?

He looked as if he was chewing on a mouthful of

tintacks. 'I don't approve, but you've got these kids to thank.'

Jeepers, that'd give him a belly-ache!

'Well done, then, the youngsters! Well done indeed.' The messenger shook all their hands. 'Firewoman Liz McKenzie. I saw you before.' She shook Josie's hand again.

'Josie Turner – an' we're the East Side Gang Fire Brigade...'

'Auxiliary auxiliaries! Then I can get back and report the bridge open – we've got two pumps waiting back there...'

Arthur, Shirley and Squib Purret from the Jubilees started re-loading the box-cart with full buckets from the basin, Eddie re-stowed the stirrup pump, while Charlie re-coiled the rope and slung it over his shoulder again, not minding the wet. Josie looked at her crew. They all seemed to be stopping their faces from smiling; grim, determined, like real AFS men and women.

'Good stuff!' she said.

Liz the messenger rode off, and keeping their heads down under the bombing, Josie and the crew ran back to Wilson's Wharf, to be ready for their next call-out. But before diving inside again she shouted up at Len on the roof.

'The East Side Gang's in business! What d'you think of that?'

But when he shouted down it wasn't a reply for her but a call-out for Dougie Raynor and his crew. 'Askew's! Filbert Street, big sheet of fire up the side.'

Everywhere outside was grey smoke and dust, with a stiff breeze blowing sparks and splinters all over – into eyes and noses and lungs. It was a relief to get in through the shelter doorway.

'Someone give you a hosing, Jose?' It was Jimmy, who must have got away from the stables. The sight of him gave her a lift. He winked at her as they passed on the stairs. 'You're sodden through, girl.'

'Saved the Bus Depot bridge!'

'Did you now? Well, that deserves a reward. Tell you what – dry yourself off an' you've won yourself a ride on Topper tomorrow!'

'I'll keep you to that.' She tried to sound normal but her throat had closed up – must have been the smoke getting to it.

'Quite right, why shouldn't you?' And Jimmy ran off to follow Dougie Raynor to Askew's.

P.J. and M. Askew's grocery shop on the corner of Filbert Street and Hope Place was half boarded up these days. The plate glass window on the Filbert Street side had been replaced by wood, but the Hope Street window, criss-crossed with gluey tape, was still intact. There was no 'P.J. Askew' serving behind the counter any more, he'd died a few years before the war, since when his widow Maud had been very much in charge and on her own. She wouldn't trust having anyone else helping in the shop, no 'bits of girls', not with food in such short supply – so customers just had to wait in line. The queue usually went out of the door and along the pavement because in this run of streets most people were registered with her for their groceries. She often gave 'tick' – everything people owed written in pencil in her little red notebook. At night she slept under the mahogany counter next to an old Swazi war club; if a bomb blast caved in the shop door no one was going to loot from Maud Askew.

But tonight it wasn't the door but the boarded-up window that was the problem. An incendiary bomb had fallen onto the paving in Filbert Street and was sending flames all over the window repair, which was a large sheet of hardboard. The flames were already threatening the wooden fascia of the guttering and in no time the roof would be on fire.

Maud was throwing buckets of water at the window from inside, but she wasn't winning. Running out to her kitchen for refills gave time for the scorching hardboard to dry and reignite...when suddenly these kids were there, shouting through the window, one of them pumping a stirrup like mad and others coming in through the shop door with buckets and tins of sand.

'Thank God! Some help.'

'Where's the kitchen, missus? Where's your water tap?'

'Out the back, where'd you think?'

There were five of them, and while some ran for water, a big fat boy started uncapping bottles of lemonade from one of her crates, fizzing them at the blaze.

'Oi! That's stock!'

But the one who looked the most sensible grabbed her tall stepladder from behind the counter and ran it at the burning hardboard. Three good runs and he'd knocked the whole thing out into the street, the fire flat on the pavement, to be trodden by the others to ash and splinters.

'That's done for it, missus.'

He was a boy from one of the Irish families. 'Thank you, son. Thank you all.'

There was water, soot, smoke everywhere – but the fire was out and the premises had been saved. And now the police were here: PC Bert Devonshire standing in the doorway, looking at the mess. Maud told him what had happened – and how the Irish boy had used his loaf.

'Well done, son. Good work, lads.' He nodded around at them all. 'But don't overstretch yourselves. Remember, anything bigger than incendiaries an' it's the AFS...'

'Come on, lads.' Already, Dougie Raynor was leading his crew out of the shop.

'We'll get the Rescue and Demolition boys in first

thing tomorrow, board you up again.' And before Maud Askew could ask him, he added, 'And I'll be here or here-about all tonight to keep an eye on the place…'

'Thank you, Bert. And there'll be a little drop of Martell if you pop your head round the door.'

'Not on duty, ma'am.' But his voice had a sort of 'uh-hum' in it.

The raid went on for two more hours, and Jimmy was on his way home after three further 'shouts'. Four hours' sleep at the most and he'd be back at the stables for the early feed. But he whistled as he walked. A faint sun was fighting the smoke from the docks beyond King Henry's Wharf. He turned the corner into Edison Street and started feeling for his door key, but round the corner to face him came the policeman from Askew's.

'It's the Irish boy again, isn't it?'

'It's the Arm of the Law once more.'

'You're right. It is. An' a nice job you did for Mrs Askew. Saved her bacon.'

'Good.' Jimmy was standing light on the balls of his feet. 'Ta. But if you'll excuse me I've got an early start, got to get to my bed.'

'Certainly. You grab what kip you can…'

Jimmy turned away.

'But not up for grabbing anything else, are we?' Suddenly the policeman's hand was on Jimmy's shoulder. 'That pocket there's got a bulge to it that doesn't look normal…'

'Sorry. What's your meaning?'

'This pocket here.' PC Devonshire's other hand was at Jimmy's left pocket. 'Like to turn it out?'

'It's only bits an' pieces. String. Rags for gripping hot bits…'

'Let's have a look, then.' The policeman stuck his hand into the pocket and did pull out a rag. But wrapped inside it weren't bits and pieces of string but a paper cone of sugar. 'Chuck this on the flames, do you?'

'Well – who's put that in there?' Jimmy looked truly puzzled. 'The shop lady, as I run out? Must have slipped it to me, like a sort of thank you…'

'Shall we go back and ask her?'

But it seemed as if the policeman knew Jimmy's answer to that. Already he had his notebook out.

'Name?'

'Jimmy Riley. Not James, an' not Seamus. Seamus was an uncle an' a real bad ha'penny.'

'Address?'

'Edison Street. Number thirteen.'

'Unlucky for some. Well, I've got this on record, Jimmy Riley. And this sugar's going back to Mrs Askew, from where it came.' He let go of Jimmy's shoulder. 'And I've got your number, son. Got it good.' He flapped his notebook in Jimmy's face. 'Now you get off home, and don't give me any more grief.'

Jimmy went, flat-footed now. But he turned to watch the policeman go – who hadn't walked back up Filbert Street towards Mrs Askew's shop, but on towards the police station, where no doubt they'd be drinking sweet tea with their breakfasts in the morning.

# 9

'It's all about balance, Jose – duckin' an' weavin', not letting 'em tell which way you're comin'…' As soon as she'd been old enough to know left from right Josie's dad had taught her how to look after herself. For him, left and right was never about her shoes or which hand she used for her pencil, but about fists. Defence. Attack. His eyes wouldn't blink as he showed her how to put up her dukes. 'No boy's got to take a'vantage of you, girl.' And they didn't dare, not while he was around, and not now that he was away. But the best of it was, he taught her how to be a winner – and it always came back to '*Balance – that's your secret.*' And balance was what she learned. When she was four he'd pushed her fast on her little two-wheeler and after a couple of wobbles she'd pedalled on without need for a hand on the saddle. And as soon as he reckoned her arms were strong enough he'd taken her out to Epping Forest on the back of his motorbike. They'd head for High Beeches where she'd watch as he did a few circuits round and round the cinder speedway track at the back of the pub; but the best bit was when she got up behind him and he raced them through the trees, and then swap places for her to ride them both, twisting the throttle and leaning into the turns.

And now all that stuff worked with Topper. When

she was up behind Jimmy, gypsy-fashion, no saddle, no stirrups, she knew where to put her weight and how to balance herself to the rhythm of the horse.

Jimmy kept his promise. In his dinner break they rode to the nearest open space, the King George Memorial Park, stopping off at the barge for Josie to check it was still the Hermits' HQ and not an exploded tin can.

It was still at its old angle, too heavy and stuck in mud to alter much whatever the tide. 'It seems OK.'

'So this is where you hang out sometimes?'

'Used to.' She pulled her frock down where it had ridden up her legs and patted Jimmy's shoulder to go.

In the park she stood and watched as he jumped Topper over a couple of flower beds. He was a real horseman, head and shoulders low over Topper's neck, hands firm on the reins, heels kicking the horse's flanks at the precise second for a jump. He raced around a litter bin and came galloping towards her like a Derby winner.

'Should've put a pound on your nose!'

'Your turn, then.' He slid off, cupped his hands, and gave her a leg up.

She wriggled herself comfortable, legs dangling, got her balance and murmured into Topper's ear the way Jimmy did. 'Steady, boy, steady.' She nudged him forward with her heels, urged him into a trot, and took him down the park. It felt good, it felt natural, only her second or third time but as if she'd been doing this for ever. Topper knew her voice and he seemed to trust her so she urged him on a bit faster. She cantered around one flower bed, then another, holding the reins tight like Jimmy and her head low against the horse's neck; and seeing him with his arms folded as if he was waiting for her to fall off, she pushed the horse into a gallop. This was great! Stoo-pendous! This was like one of those times in Epping Forest riding on the AJS, it made her feel light in the head and happy. She looked up and around. Over to her right and halfway back to Jimmy there was a park bench. Well, what could she do with that? It was no more than a polished plank about a foot-and-a-half off the ground, not high, had no back. Easy, or not?

She decided to go for it; her first ever jump. She pulled the reins to the right, heading Topper for it.

'Oi!' Jimmy's arms weren't folded any more, he was waving them wildly across himself.

But she shut her eyes to that, she'd got to concentrate, measure her distance before her crucial kick. 'Come on, boy! We can do it, we can do it!' With her forehead down on the horse's neck she straightened him up and gee'ed him on towards the bench, well-balanced, reining him tight, holding him on course, being the boss.

'*Josie!*' Jimmy was running to cut her off but he wouldn't make it.

Would Topper baulk? Would he twist away and try

to go around? Would he throw her? No. She gave him two digs with her heels and he galloped at the bench, lowered his head and with a final kick from her he took off, up and over, landing sure-footed on the other side to take her galloping on down the park.

It had been like flying. 'Good boy! Good Topper! You done it!'

She slowed him to a canter, then a trot and a walk, smiling proudly down at Jimmy – who grabbed the reins and pulled her off.

'Idiot mare, you! You could have broke a fetlock, had to have him put down. You weren't heavens-high over that bench, you missed the thing by inches. *Inches!*' He backed off, then suddenly took a run at Topper and mounted. 'Jumping with no saddle and stirrups, you're mad! You could've gone over his head an' broke your neck.'

'Would you be sorry, then?' She had defiance in her eyes but an apologetic sort of mouth.

'Not a lot!' With a twist of his head Jimmy rode out of the park – leaving her to walk home, asking herself all the way, what could have got into the boy? She was proud of herself, her dad would've been proud of her, but something was up with Jimmy Riley because he should have been proud of her today. He'd kept last night's promise and given her a ride on Topper, but when she thought about it there'd been no winks, no smiles, no blarney. Most other times he'd have seen what she'd done and jumped Topper again himself, just to show how much higher he could go.

Yes, he was definitely different today, and she reckoned it wasn't about the no saddles, no stirrups, or broken necks. And she found herself not feeling so much angry with him as sorry for him.

Although it was still a long slog back to Monks Street.

That night the raiders came over again, as predictable as the tide. At Wilson's Wharf the East Side Gang were all there. Ivy had left Josie with Auntie Varley and a 'Be good!' while she went off to another shelter with Freddie Fowler's 'Not Downhearted' concert party. But even with Ivy off the scene Josie kept her crew lying low for a while – because Len was off the roof tonight, swapping fire-watching duties with Sonny Bailey so he could see some action for himself. And he could be a right pain when he tried to come the big brother.

Her other problem had been Sonny's dad. He knew what her crew had done at the wooden bridge – so what if he told her mum? Had he changed his tune after the last few days since he'd seen what kids could do? She reckoned he must have, because he'd been in and out of the shelter several times while Ivy was there and he'd never said a word. Like a few other people these days he didn't seem to be treating her like a little kid, which was good. Anyhow, she'd keep her fingers crossed.

The first shout soon came down.

'Back of Saunders' Leather Works.'

Josie had to smile as Len led off Sonny's crew, pointing his iron bar like a soldier leading his men into battle. 'Come on, lads, we can smell our way there!'

'Should've brung our gas masks, we'll be up to our necks in you-know-what.'

The back of the leather works was where they used pee and dung to tan the hides – always a high old stink. A good miss of a call-out, Josie reckoned. But she knew the East Side Gang wouldn't be next, not after putting one over on Dougie Raynor the night before. They'd be picking up pieces again.

'Keep us a bit clear, can't you?' Micky wasn't a bad sort, but the last few nights he'd been getting ratty with kids blocking the aisles. 'Move right down the car, please!'

Early on there was no sign of Jimmy; but Josie knew he wasn't likely to turn up before Elijah got back from the infirmary. If he turned up at all, the funny boy. There'd been something up with him today, no doubt about that.

It was quieter overhead now; the bombing of the local docks seemed to have happened when the first raiders flew upriver.

'Come on, let's have a butcher's outside.' She headed

her crew towards the steps. 'Get out for a breath of air, see what we can see. Check the state of our bridge.'

They waited while Arthur did a wee on the way. He was one of those boys who suddenly had to go, his face wincing up with anxiety. Luckily they were near the bushes in Victoria Gardens a few yards along the street. Josie's mother always reckoned the place was like the grounds of an asylum, a small open space with trees and shrubs where old men sat behind high railings.

'Give it a quick shake, Arf, or they'll keep you in.'

When they came to the bridge it was fine. They stamped and jumped on the fresh wood of the repair. Fire engines could get to the dock without having to slow down, thanks to the East Side Gang; which made Josie want another call-out, to prove they were still worth their salt.

'Come on, let's see what's happening back at HQ.' And Jimmy might have turned up by now.

She set them off – and heard the shouting long before they'd gone far. It came from the waterfront alley next to the London River pub. Running past it they were almost knocked off their feet by drinkers coming out of the cellar and scooting off in all directions.

'A bomb!'

'On the spit!'

'Goin' off any second!'

'Gawd help us!'

'Leg it!'

And then: 'Hang on – we've got ropes…'

And that voice sounded like Len's – the leather works must have been a quick job. She'd got to see what was going on here. She pushed through the drinkers and ran along the alley towards the Captain Lowry Stairs.

And stopped.

'Jeepers!'

There it was, down on the spit of sand – a long black bomb lying on its side, about the same size as a man, one end pointed and the other end just half a fin, all bent and twisted. *Crikey!* She'd never seen an actual bomb, and here was this monster stuck half in and half out of the sand. And with Len leaning over it tying a length of rope around the broken fin.

'We'll drag it into the river.'

Her *stupid* brother! 'Len! Watch out! Could be a time bomb!' It was one thing him squirting a stirrup pump, something different tying a rope to a bomb that could blow him to smithereens. 'Leave it, Len!'

'Whole bally pub'll go if that blows up!' The landlord was down there, but not helping – keeping his distance, the yellow-belly.

'*Leave it, Len! Run away!*' She couldn't shout it any louder.

But Len took no notice, he stayed bending there making sure of the roping.

'*Leave it!*' Josie's throat hurt with screeching.

He was putting his ear to the bomb. 'It's not ticking – it's a dud.' He put another loop around the fin. 'It'll be bloomin' heavy! I'll need a few hands.'

'Not after it blows up you won't!' Josie ran down the stairs to drag him away. But the landlord grabbed at her, and held her, kicking and twisting.

'Let him finish.'

'That's my brother!'

'An' he'll be done in seconds. Look out there!'

She looked out at the river. Heading for the spit was a lighterage tug fitted up as an emergency fire brigade boat with a fireman shouting through a loud-hailer.

'How much rope you got? Get it out to us! We'll come in as close as we can!'

'Enough.' Len had finished his knotting.

'Get back! Get back!' Now the Bus Depot warden was there, clearing the alley and the stairs. As he came down onto the spit Josie ran along under the river wall, ready to drag at Len if he didn't get back quickly.

But Len wasn't getting back at all, he was wading out towards the fire-boat with the rope, where a fireman was waist deep in the water coming to meet him. Tying his own thicker rope to Len's, the fireman turned to shout at the tug. 'Make ready to go astern! Full speed, out to deeper water.'

'Aye, aye, Chief!'

'And you get back and duck your head,' the fireman shouted at Len. 'Dead unstable, these!' He smacked Len on the back and waded towards the tug as the slack of the rope began being taken up.

Josie didn't want to watch, but she had to. Going by how much rope the tug had paid out she could see the good distance the firemen were putting between them and the bomb, which was a heck more of a distance than Len had.

*'Come back quick, Len! Get back here!'*

The tug notched up its engine and with a crack the rope tightened and sent spray into the air. The bomb shifted a bit on the spit. But what would moving it do? With high revs the tug went into 'fast astern', Len still wading for shore as the bomb started to be dragged across the sand. *Would this be it?*

Josie screeched again: *'Hurry! Hurry!'* Len's shortest way to safety was past the bomb as it scraped across shingle at the water's edge. *'Run like heck!'* And she'd kill that coward landlord one day, who was charging up the stairs with his hands over his head.

Another notch up of its engine and the tug was moving out fast towards mid-river – but what was this? *God help Len!* A loop of the rope must have caught round his ankle because suddenly he was thrown off his feet and being dragged out ahead of the bomb.

*'Stop! Stop!'* Dodging the warden Josie ran for the

water. *'Tug! Come back!'* But the firemen on the tug couldn't see how Len was flat in the water, splashing desperately as he tried to free himself.

*'Stop it! Come back! Slacken off! Let him loose!'*

Josie's wasn't the only voice. Everyone on shore could see what was happening and they shouted and yelled and waved as they watched Len fighting to get himself free.

*'Len!'* She ran into the water out towards her brother. To see him go under, come up, and go under again.

*'Len! Len!'*

And with a last weak wave of his arms he went under once more – for five seconds, ten seconds, thirty seconds, a minute – and didn't show again.

*'Jesus Christ!'*

And Josie's piercing, mournful shriek could be heard across the water and all along King Henry's Wharf. A screeched lament for Len Turner. Her brother. Drowned in the Thames to save the bleeding London River pub.

# 10

Josie slept with Len's iron bar under her pillow. When Ivy had come back from the concert party and wailed at the terrible news, she and Josie had walked every inlet and creek of the river until they'd argued about which way Len could have been taken by the turning tide. They split up, and Josie had gone back to the Lowry Stairs in the mad hope of seeing Len come walking out of the water; but such a thought was like the wisp of a fading dream because of course there was no Len – although his iron bar was there, down in the rubbish at the water's edge. So she'd grabbed it, dried it, taken it home and kept it secret.

Len's body was recovered not far downriver. Ivy claimed him from the public mortuary and had him laid out in his coffin in their front room: peaceful, and cold. But if Len lay there looking young and trouble-free, Josie saw her mother change from a woman with tons of 'go' to a red-eyed, nervy wreck. And where on a fine day the sun had come into their house, their curtains were now drawn in a twenty-four-hour blackout.

There was no chance of Private Turner coming home from the Far East, and Josie had felt herself changing from being Ivy's daughter to a sort of sister. She'd helped her word the letter to her dad, gone with Ivy to the

Births, Marriages and Deaths office, and helped choose Len's coffin at Daley's Undertakers. Now she made pots of tea for visitors to his laying-out, and queued for rations when all Ivy wanted to do was sit with Len in the dark. And every night between the drowning and Len's funeral, when the siren went they both stayed in the house with him, taking their chances.

And she listened to Ivy saying it over and over and over again. *'Silly sod. Silly brave sod. Tying a bit of rope to a ruddy bomb!'*

Most of the Turners and Ivy's Walker side of the family were buried in the Borough Cemetery, dotted about in different plots wherever there'd been a space at the time. And space was what was needed for Len's burial. So many turned out for it that they were standing between, behind, and on the kerbs of graves, eight and nine deep. As Tony Milner said, 'He had a damn good turn-out.' All Len's mates were there: old school pals, dockers, the football team, and the Dead End Kids. There was a Walker gran and two Turner aunts, and a cousin in army uniform from Aldershot. There were neighbours from streets around, old George Knight and Lou Sutton from the Globe, and a crew of off-watch AFS men from Stepney Street fire station; and, in her uniform, Liz the motorbike messenger as well.

Josie stood next to Ivy who was in the deepest shade

of black, her face hidden under a heavy veil as the coffin was lowered slowly into the ground. And as it went down out of sight Josie's stomach twisted at the sudden, awful thought that she and the rest of them would go home when this was over, and Len would be left down there on his own. But she wasn't going to do what she wanted to do, and cry. For Ivy's sake she was going to keep her wailing inside.

The vicar gave Ivy a handful of earth to throw down onto the coffin. '*Earth to earth, ashes to ashes, dust to dust…*' Ivy stepped solemnly forward and threw the earth into the grave. She bowed her head and said something quiet and private. Now Josie wanted to throw a handful of earth, too, but before she could move forward Ivy suddenly stood away from the edge of the grave, threw her veil back over her hat, and turned to face Len's Dead End Kids.

'It's got to stop!' She didn't shout it, didn't mumble it in grief, she said it out clearly as if she'd got a pub microphone in her hand. 'All you kids! Running around with prams and barrows and bits and pieces of half-useless tat. Pretending to do firemen's work. But you're not trained for any of that, you're not old enough or strong enough – and if you carry on the way you're going they'll start thinking they don't need the real people any more.' She pointed into the grave and swung round at the AFS fire crew. 'Not your fault – but my Len got

**114**

killed doing your job! A big kid, hardly out of school.'
And, twisting round to Len's crews again, 'But you get
back to being kids. And stay kids, or there won't be
no next generation to carry on the East End.' She
stood there as if she was about to say some more, but
she suddenly pulled down her veil like a curtain falling,
stood to attention, and gave Len's grave a proud
soldiers' salute.

Josie picked her moment and took Ivy's elbow. 'Come
on, Mum.' Just as another hand took hers.

'I'm sorry, Jose. Sorry I wasn't there that night.' It was
Jimmy Riley, wearing a pressed jacket, white shirt and
black tie; the trouble he'd taken for Len.

'Cheers, Jimmy.'

He backed away for her to lead Ivy from the graveside
to the cemetery gates. As they waited for the cars to
arrive people came up and paid their respects. One of
them was Liz the motorbike messenger, who took Josie
aside. 'Bide your time, lassie. The boys at the station were
full of Len Turner and what he was doing.' She lowered
her voice. 'You're needed, everyone's needed, and as soon
as you're the age I'll see to it you get your legs over a
motorbike…'

Josie kept a still face, but what a lift that would have
been on a normal day.

Daley's cars drew up to take the family back to
Hermitage Quays and their front room in Monks Street,

where Josie was shocked to see plates of sandwiches on the table where Len's coffin had lain, as if it had never been there.

Which choked her. He had gone. This really was 'Goodbye Len'.

'No being rude to your mum, but she's wrong – we've got to carry on.'

Josie read Sonny Bailey's face as they stood outside the greengrocers at the back of a queue for what they hadn't got – bananas, all a rumour. He was holding on to a large pram, tatty at the top but with four meaty wheels below. She ignored what he'd said, pointed into the pram's large interior. 'How many pounds o' bananas are you not gonna buy?'

'It's for the wheels, stupid.'

''Course. Where'd you get it?'

At first Sonny looked as if he wasn't going to tell her. 'Burdett Road Station. Had my pick. Yesterday's council evacuation, the mums took their kids to the station but the railway people wouldn't let the prams on the trains, so they had to leave them outside.'

'Really? Many left?'

'A few. Council's collecting them.'

'Then I'll get down there quick.'

He twisted up his mouth. 'So you think like I do?'

'About what?'

'What I said. Carrying on. Not giving up on the Dead End Kids.'

Josie kicked one of his pram wheels as if she was testing its tyre pressure. She was going to make him say the next thing, although she guessed what it was going to be.

'I can take over. Run the Dead End Kids. I was Len's number two, wasn't I?'

'Oh, was you?' She stuck her tongue in her cheek.

'Well, who else is there – good at organising and running things?'

She put her head on one side. 'Don't you know?'

She could see by his frown he was ticking off names in his head, Dougie, Ray, perhaps even Jimmy. 'Well, who?'

'You're looking at her.'

'*You?*' His grip slipped on the pram handle and it tried to get away. 'But you've already got your lot. Your East Side Gang.' He pulled the pram back, put on its brake, and stood up facing her straight. 'I've had a word with Raynor and Gull and Brewer, and they'll fall in behind me, they've said so.'

Josie was standing tall, too. Very tall. 'Oh, will they? Well, I won't, son, because I'm in this an' all. All right, Len wouldn't have let me, but there's no one to stop me now.'

Sonny Bailey shrugged his shoulders, as if to say *we'll see about that.*

'And you don't know it – but I've got Len's iron bar. He never went to work without it, and the Dead End Kids was his work, an' all. His iron bar's the leader's, everyone respects that – so anyone who wants it has got to get it off me.'

Sonny laughed in her face. 'Off you?'

'Off me.'

He snorted. 'A girl? How? Buy it? Toss for it? Go to your mum and ask her to make you hand it over?'

Josie stared him in the face. 'No, Sonny, nothing like that. Something dead easy. Right up your street, as it goes.'

'Oh? What's that?'

'Fight me. Fight me for it. Whoever wants it, whoever wants to be chief of the Dead End Kids is gonna have to fight me for Len's iron bar…'

'Oh, boy!' He laughed in her face again.

'An' I'll talk to Raynor and the others an' include them an' all. I'll take you all on – one at a time, o' course.'

'I'm not fighting a girl.'

'Then you've lost 'fore you start, haven't you? Them kids respect what Len's iron bar means, an' they won't have some grammar school boy getting it on the toss of a threepenny bit.'

Sonny cleared his throat, eyed her up. 'Can't be boxing, though, can it, 'cos of your being…' He nodded at her chest.

'Don't worry about me. You keep your hand on your ha'penny, that's all. It's no holds barred. All-in.' She lifted her chin at him. 'All right?'

'All right?' He giggled. 'Me against you? I'll say all right.'

'Good.' Looking the other way she suddenly kicked the brake off his pram and gave it a push along the pavement. 'See you, Sonny. I'm off down the station. My Dead End Kids'll need a few spare wheels.' And she went. But, 'Bananas!' she called back from the corner. 'That's you, Bailey – thinking you can always get what you want!'

# 11

The location was kept as secret as a bare-knuckle bout. No one who could stop the contest was to get wind of it – and definitely not Bill Bailey or Ivy Turner. Word went quietly around the Dead End Kids and the East Side Gang, and only them.

Tony Milner found the place – and Josie went along with another good idea he had: getting someone neutral and respected to be in charge on the night, like old George Knight, loyal from the start to Len and the Dead End Kids. For a mouthy boy, Josie reckoned, Tony Milner sometimes showed a bit of sense. And his fighting ground was a peach.

The Methodist chapel in Timber Street was small and tinny, but it had a hut at the back which was used for Scouts, Guides, Cubs and Brownies – and Tony Milner's mother did chapel cleaning so she had a set of keys. And the treacle on the pudding was, no one used the hut on Thursdays.

The fight had to wait until after work. Sonny had defied his father and got himself an office-boy job at the *Stepney Advertiser*. And because George Knight had agreed to see fair play, the fight couldn't start before the big film went on at the Globe.

Josie chose what she'd wear very carefully: slacks and

a long-sleeved roll-neck sweater, school shoes with the metal tips, and a tightly tied turban so Sonny couldn't pull her hair. She reckoned she looked like a sailor off one of the lascar ships.

There was a gate at the side of the chapel leading round to the hut, and the keys Tony Milner had filched opened both. Josie thought she was getting there early, but most of the Dead End Kids were already standing or sitting on the lockers running along the walls. As she walked in it all went quiet; she could almost hear the sound of breath being held. Looking at their faces she couldn't tell which side people were on. Shirley – yes, she'd be up for a girl leader – but she couldn't be sure about any of the boys other than Arthur, Eddie, and probably Charlie Drew and Squib. She knew there'd be plenty behind Sonny and there'd be others who'd play it safe – wait and see and not shout for either of them till there was a winner. But the big question in her head was: if Jimmy Riley came, whose side would he be on?

She sat next to Arthur on a Girl Guide locker, along from an empty flagpole in the corner.

'Should've brought our Hermit flag off the barge. Run it up the pole when you...' But Arthur didn't finish what he was saying, because just then Sonny Bailey strutted in, flanked by Dougie Raynor and Ray Gull, all three making an entrance as if they were at the Empire Ring. Spotting Josie, Sonny went to the opposite side of the hut, standing with his feet apart and his arms folded across his chest.

'You want to sit down for a few minutes, Bailey,' Josie called over. ''Fore your legs go wobbly. Be easy enough to get you down as it is.' Now she'd got him stuck with standing there like that, and a proper twerp he looked, too, all stiff and showing off. She stared at Raynor and Gull standing like loyal guards on either side of him. She was going to be their leader, and they could get used to it or get out of the Dead End Kids as quick as they liked.

Sonny turned to look at the kids down each side of the hut. 'I'm not happy to be fighting a girl,' he said, 'but she will have it – so don't make yourselves comfortable, I'll get it over quick.' He sniffed and tossed his head back with a cocky shake.

'No hanging on in the clinches, Sonny!' At which Bert Brewer got a laugh – just as George Knight came in to a cheer: white shirt, waistcoat with watch and fob, and in his hand a yellow duster wrapped around something solid.

He picked out Tony Milner. 'Got a table, son?'

Tony Milner unfolded a card table from behind the flagpole, which George put near the door. He carefully laid down the yellow duster, spread it out on the table, and exposed Len's iron bar.

Josie sat up, her back never straighter. She'd taken the bar round to the Globe that morning, sad to let go of it, but she was definitely taking it home that night.

'This was Len Turner's.' George looked around, lifted up the bar in both hands as if it was the Lonsdale Belt. He laid it down again. 'Len always carried it as leader of the Dead End Kids, and it stands for the leader's authority. So at the end of tonight anyone who doesn't respect the new leader's right to carry it – male or female – is gonna get a clonk over the head from me.' He picked the bar up again, hit it on the table, and let it drop. 'OK?'

Every face in the hut showed how that was OK.

'I'm not sure about mixed male and female fighting, but my Lou reckons Josie's got to have her equal chance if she wants it; and she does want it. Now, before we commence…'

'Gawd, get on with it, George!' Josie stood up. 'Look at Bailey, he's gone white as a sheet. I don't want to win by a technical faint.' She walked into the centre of the hut, looked around at everyone. 'This is gonna be an all-in fight. Last man on her feet's the winner. Right?'

Sonny Bailey dropped his arms, worked his fists like a gorilla grabbing, and took two steps towards her.

'Hold on!' George was having the last word before this started. With one hand up to hold everyone still, with the other he put his football referee's whistle to his lips and gave a short, sharp blast. 'After the start, when I blow this, you both stop. Whatever's happening, you stop. Right?'

'Right.' But Sonny Bailey's voice came out as more of a croak.

Josie nodded and jumped into a wrestling position, which Bailey quickly copied. She danced sideways, came back. He did the same, each staring the other in the eyes.

George Knight came round to the front of the table and stood ready himself. 'Seconds out! Ding-ding.' He blew his whistle.

And the fight began.

Josie knew Sonny was nervous about her being a girl, wouldn't want to punch her where he shouldn't, so he'd probably go for wrestling over boxing. And from where he was looking at her waist she guessed he was going to make a sudden grab there, try to get a leg behind hers and throw her down. She'd got her own plan, though; she was going to beat him at his own game, but by talking about 'getting him down' she had deliberately got him expecting her to wrestle. Well, whichever way things ended up, she wasn't going to disappoint him.

She kept her feet moving – forwards, backwards, sideways, circling him, as if looking for a good hand-hold. He was keeping his arms wide just below his chest, ready to go for a grab around her middle – so she'd got to be ready to counter that. But attack was better than defence so she'd go higher, get at his neck, stick her fingers down the collar of his shirt, grip it tight, and yank his head sideways. Then she could curl her foot behind him, pull him to the floor and jump on top of him – face down, face up, she didn't care which. She'd shout, 'Got you, Bailey!' and let him up while she skipped around the floor – because she didn't want a quick wrestling win, she wanted the world to see that she'd licked him good and proper at his own game.

*Now!*

She darted in, looked as if she was going for his waist so his arms came down, then she suddenly grabbed at his neck. But he was quicker than she was. He was a District boxer, light on his feet, knew his stuff, and instantly he was skipping back out of reach. And because she couldn't stop her lunge, he let her come on, rugby-tackled her, and down she went.

*Blast!*

In seconds he was sitting on her and suddenly the hut erupted. The Sonny Bailey boys whistled and the East Siders shouted as the two of them fought it out on the floor, locked and squirming, Sonny's sneering face thrust into hers saying, 'Got you! Got you! Got you!' Breathing hard, he shifted his position to bring his knees up onto her shoulders, going for the pin-down, *one, two, three!* God, this was going to be over so fast, just like he'd said.

Unless… All at once she went limp and let go the pressing-up at his shoulders which suddenly changed the balance of their bodies; now she could just about get one of her hands cupped under his chin. She pushed two fingers upwards as if she was going to shove them up his nose – which took his head back and lost him his concentration for a split second – when she brought her knee up hard in Sonny's groin. Really hard.

'Grrrmph!'

'Sorry!'

She could see he was trying to ride the pain while keeping up his pressure on her shoulders; so she kneed him again, different knee, same groin.

'Oooff!' And he had to pull off.

*Thank you, Len!* He'd told her to do that if she was ever attacked – *'And do it like you mean it.'* Well, she had.

'Cheat, Turner!'

'Getting my legs free. Said sorry!'

She was on her feet fast and so was he, trying to focus his watering eyes. *Good enough!* she reckoned. He might have got her down, but he hadn't won his wrestling victory – so now she was going to beat him the way she'd planned. Jumping into her dad's boxing stance she put up her fists and danced around him, prodding at his head with her right.

'She's going bare-knuckle. She's after the old K.O.'

'Nah. Girls can't box.'

'See my mum!'

No one had expected this, especially Sonny Bailey, but the smile coming on his face said that was all right by him. He was District boxing champion and he was good, this was going to be a walkover. She'd played into his hands. He started shuffling lightly around her, all professional, nifty footwork getting a few cheers, his eyes focused, his chin down, his arms working, his guard well up. She might be a girl, but he still had plenty to aim at with her head and shoulders and her solar plexus.

But he was stiffer than she was. He was 'schoolboy boxing' trained the same as Len, he'd followed a step-by-step progression through the Boys' Club boxing manual – while her dad's work-outs had been in rough halls and fairground booths: *'Come on, lads, win a fiver off the Champ'* – and once or twice he had. *Balance, always balance and a good defence*, yes, but he'd trained her to attack in his rough-house way, arms sometimes hanging loose to bring the opponent on, then suddenly using the Turner secret weapon. *Doing the switch.*

Bailey came at her, jabbing, his feet shuffling forward. Still boxing orthodox, she gave ground, kept her head back. He'd go for her head or her bread basket, not her chest: well, more fool him; as far as she was concerned 'all-in' meant 'all-in'.

And he landed one. He was quick, snake-quick, and out of nowhere he caught her a stinger on the side of her face.

'Ha!'

But it fired her. *Right! Now!* As he came in for the kill she suddenly did the switch. She jumped her feet, changed her balance, swapped orthodox for southpaw, brought up her left fist to do the work of the right. Her dad's words: '*It throws 'em, they don't know how to counter.*' She jerked her head aside to avoid a punch on the other cheek, and now he looked cocky and puzzled both at once, shook his head to show everyone how stupid she was – girls' silly fighting – which for a vital second lost him his concentration again and gave her the chance to elbow in under his guard. And from an unexpected direction that he couldn't defend, she brought up her left fist and landed a hard uppercut under his nose.

*Squidge!*

It was good, it would have been a nose-breaker if he hadn't jerked his head back in the nick of time; but he was in real trouble, blood was pouring out of him onto the floor, and before George could get his whistle to his mouth Josie moved in like lighting and one, two – still southpaw – she gave him a third to the stomach – *guff!* – and caught him with a beaut of a right-hander smack on the point of his chin.

Down he went – not flat on the canvas but in a heap on the floorboards, looking like a bundle of clothes for the rag man.

'One, two, three…' Arthur and the East Side Gang started the knock-out count, and a lot of the others joined in. *Josie Turner had won!* She had Sonny Bailey's sweat on her sleeves and his blood on her knuckles, but she had won, squarely if not quite fairly.

'Eight, nine, ten!' George Knight lifted her arm as the victor, and he signalled for Tony Milner to look after Sonny. And while the loser was leant against a locker George picked up the iron bar and put it into Josie's hands: the symbol of leadership last held by Len Turner at the Captain Lowry Stairs – now being presented to her as the winner of the contest.

'I give this into the hands of Josie Turner, the new leader of the Dead End Kids. And that's the end of the competition.' George Knight looked around the hut, and he must have caught sight of a doubtful eye. 'Listen, son – if you know your history you know their names: Queen Elizabeth; Boadicea: strong women; Joan of Arc, good leader, strong girl. And tons of other women not famous but who you definitely wouldn't argue with…'

'My mum again!'

'Yes!' George swung round towards the voice. 'And my Lou. So now you've got your Josie Turner. Right? Anyone got any argument with that?'

No one had – and especially not the boy who'd just lit up Josie's eyes. Jimmy Riley, over by the door, who must have been there in time to see her beating Sonny Bailey.

He gave her a wink and a thumbs-up. 'Well done, Jose. An' if you want a number two, remember, I'm your fellow.'

No one looked as if they wanted to argue with that, either. And the moment was right. As the air-raid siren sounded the alert Josie raised the iron bar and pointed it around the hut.

'So it's everyone to the shelter, an' fast. Dead End Kids – we've got stuff to do tonight.'

The hut emptied quickly. 'You in or out?' she shouted at Sonny Bailey. What sort of loser would he be?

He was groggy; he'd been spark out for half a minute, and his nose was still dripping blood. But he was plucky – and she'd guessed he would be. His dad would stick at things to the end even though he was a pain in the backside – and Sonny was the same sort. And trained in the schoolboy boxing world like Len had been, he knew how to take losing as well as winning.

'Don't worry about me.'

'Does that mean…?'

'Said, don't worry.' He kept up with her.

She put on a spurt. 'You go lookout for tonight, then. And Jimmy – you run Sonny's crew.'

'Aye-aye, Skipper.'

And at the sound of that she looked around at the others. 'An' don't none of you forget it, neither.'

# 12

Josie never took Ivy for a fool – nobody ever got one over on Ivy Turner, not even Josie's dad. But a lot of these nights she was out at other shelters with Freddie Fowler's concert party, and on a Saturday she'd do her regular turn at the Pirate, so Josie had a fair amount of freedom without having to try too many tricks. But Ivy was sometimes in the shelter with the rest and Josie had to play things cleverly. Occasionally she'd decide to delegate the iron bar to Arthur or Charlie and miss a call-out, but when she did she'd stick closer to Ivy than she liked and soon get sent packing. 'You don't want to hear all our old talk, you're getting too knowing, my girl.' But indoors after the All Clear Ivy could still be sniffy – literally sniffy – twitching her nose like ol' Brer Rabbit. 'Gawd, Josephine Mary, you've got the smell of smoke on you! You'd better not be into my fags!' And Josie guessed she was putting that spin on things because her Josie would never dare do what her dead Len had done, would she?

But the fire-bomb one Friday night at Auntie Beattie Bassey's seemed to make a bit of difference in Ivy's eyes.

Like a lot of the others, Auntie Beattie Bassey wasn't a real auntie, but she was very important to Ivy. She was a dressmaker who lived over Sprey's the Barber's in Palmer Street. If anyone was getting married, Auntie

Beattie did wedding dresses; if they were pregnant she let out their frocks; if there was a death in the family she could quickly run up something in black. And her importance to Ivy, now she'd retired from making stage dresses for West End shows, was sometimes giving her a new look for her singing. She was a short, plump woman with dyed red hair, 'no stranger to a ginger biscuit', who could talk and laugh through a mouthful of pins while she did a deal that Ivy couldn't turn down. Now and again it would be something new but more often it was an alteration to a dress she'd kept after a show ended. 'I've got this cut-down ball-gown, Ivy, the frock I made for Jessie Matthews in *Evergreen* – it'll just do you perfect.'

That Friday night Ivy was out with the concert party and Dougie Raynor shouted down a hit on Sprey's the Barber's; and because of Auntie Beattie Bassey living upstairs Josie made sure she led out her own team. It could be an incendiary bomb or a small explosive that had hit the electrics, but she knew that up there in Auntie Beattie's place there were racks of clothes and rolls of inflammable material: and the woman never went to a shelter. 'I'll take my chances, ducks.'

'Come on! My auntie lives on top of Sprey's!'

Shirley couldn't make it; she was being sat on by her mother. 'Sorry, Jose,' she mouthed. So Josie took big Phil Jupp, who saluted and raced them up the steps.

Palmer Street was a short row of shops, mostly boarded up these days. No one was about, least of all Mr Sprey who didn't live on the premises. But the fire wasn't in the barber's salon, it was on the other side of the partition leading up to Auntie Beattie's flat. An incendiary bomb must have come slanting down through the skylight and set light to the stairs.

When they got there Auntie Beattie was up beneath the skylight doing a frantic dance, hands cupped to her mouth and shouting at the street door. 'Help! H-e-e-e-lp! I can't get down! I can't get out!'

'All right! All right, Auntie! We'll get you down.'

'How? Look at them stairs.'

The stairs were burning. But Josie's crew quickly put out the flames: a stirrup pump and three buckets of water soon had the fire damped down, and now the main problem was gaping at them: a five- or six-stair hole, big enough to stop Auntie Beattie getting down. She could never get across that gap.

'It's all right, Auntie, the fire's done for. Sit your bum down somewhere. When the firemen come they'll have a ladder…'

'*Sit down? When they come!* Haven't you got a nose? Can't you smell the gas?'

Josie and the others took good sniffs. And she was right, a faint smell of gas was in amongst the smell of the dead fire – that sour smell everyone knew from broken mains. Josie went cold. It seemed to be getting stronger. This was no leaky oven tap, the bomb must have damaged a joint in the pipework. It was only lucky it hadn't started leaking while the fire was burning. A lucky escape – up till now! But while Josie's Dead End Kids could back off to safety, Auntie Beattie was a prisoner up there.

'It's coming on stronger! How the hell am I going to get down?'

Josie took it in. The woman couldn't jump, she'd break her legs, and there was no back way down. 'Hang on!' But the gas was building up; none of them could hang about for long. She looked at the stairs where the banisters' iron supports stuck out of the wall. If she reached them for a grip and pulled herself up she reckoned she could just get to Auntie Beattie.

'Clear off out of it, you kids! You'll all be blown to kingdom come. Leave me – just call for help! *Oh, my God, my God!*' Auntie Beattie wrapped a length of chiffon around her face.

But Josie wouldn't clear off out of it. She'd had an idea. She grabbed Charlie Drew's arm. 'Come on, Charlie, you an' me.'

'What?'

'Up! An' Eddie, cop hold of my iron bar, an' you an' Roy an' Phil stay back shining your lights till I call you forward. An' keep listening for the fire brigade.'

Josie took hold of the furthest banister supports she could reach and started pulling herself up, hand, foot, hand, foot, with Charlie close behind her.

'Get down, Josie! I told you. Save yourself, child.'

Josie ignored her. She knew this place, came here with Ivy sometimes, and she'd had an idea. When she got to the landing she dodged around Auntie Beattie and by the light of her torch she ran to the room where she kept her rolls of material.

'This stuff. Which is the heaviest?'

Auntie Beattie followed her in. 'What you on about cloth for?'

'Which is the thickest? Quick! Something strong.'

'Gawd Almighty!' Auntie Beattie picked out a bolt of chestnut wool fabric. 'Good blend, this. Thirty-six inch. Best coats only. But what the devil…?'

'Just right! Come on, Charlie.' The gas was really drifting up now. She took one end of the bolt and Charlie took the other. 'Top of the stairs.'

The bolt was a good width and would do. 'Get ready, you lot!'

At the foot of the stairs the others had wrapped Sprey's towels around their faces so their shouts back were muffled. 'Hurry up or we're gonna die!'

Auntie Beattie was pushing Josie to go. 'Save yourselves, you two! You kids can drop down that hole.' She sounded woozy from the gas, the way Josie was starting to feel as she pulled Charlie into position with her, across the top of the stairs.

'What the hell are you doing, girl?'

'It's not what I'm doing, Auntie, it's what you're doing. Goin' to do.' She held the cloth out to Charlie, sideways across the space between them. 'Grip this hard, Charlie, dig your nails in, an' hold it tight.' Copying her, Charlie did as he was told. 'You ready down there?' Bravely, the others still were. 'Now catch hold of the end of this.' On her nod she and Charlie let go of the bolt of fabric, which unrolled itself downwards, picking up speed. 'Got it?' The others grabbed at it, pulled it and straightened it. 'Now you lot hold it tight – about six inches off the stairs.'

'What's this for? Josie Turner, what're you doing?'

But now it was obvious. Josie had made a slide.

'I'm never going down that! I'm either on my feet, in my chair, or on my bed. No way do I slide down stairs on my backside!'

'It's that or get gassed up here.' Josie put on her best Ivy Turner look. ''Cos I tell you, Auntie, in two ticks Charlie an' me are clearing off out of it. We've got half the gas company in our lungs already.'

Auntie Beattie stared down – as Charlie turned his head aside and started to hiss. 'Just listen to that!'

Auntie Beattie crossed herself. 'Strewth alive!'

'Get on it, then.' Josie had never felt so much in

command, supervising Auntie Beattie in her straddle across the cloth. 'Take the strain down there!'

'What d'you mean, *strain*? Cheeky cat!'

And although Auntie Beattie wasn't that huge, it was as much as they could all do to keep the cloth tight, Josie and Charlie leaning back like sailors with a sail in a storm, all of them just about keeping the cloth clear of the stairs, and Big Phil proving his worth with his weight. 'Go! Go on!' With a smack on Auntie Beattie's grip of the banister post Josie helped make up her mind for her. 'Let rip, Auntie!'

'Whoa! Here I come, mother!'

Down went Auntie Beattie, whooping all the way – *bump, bump, bump, bump, bump*. 'Oh, my burning bum! I shan't sit down for a twelvemonth.'

The crew pulled her to her feet at the bottom and helped her to run round the corner, while Josie and Charlie clambered down the banister supports.

Now help was arriving; a Civil Defence rescue team bravely went under the stairs in case they had to plug the gas leak, but already their Chief Officer was turning off the supply in the street.

Quietly, at Auntie Beattie's pace, Josie and the others walked her towards Wilson's Wharf. 'You'll get a nice cup of tea in there…'

'Cup of tea? A jar of Vaseline and summat a bit stronger, if you don't mind. My poor arse! Me, sliding down the stairs – and on a bolt of chestnut at two-an'-six a yard! But you're a good girl, Josie, a good girl.'

'Listen, Auntie, just don't go on about me to Ivy, OK?' Josie winked at her. 'She don't know what I get up to.'

But ten minutes later, drinking tea with a drop of gin in it, Auntie Beattie worried Josie with what she said to Auntie Varley. 'Tell her mother I'm grateful for what Josie done. Tell her that girl's a real gutsy Turner. You don't win wars without the likes of people like her.'

'Gawd, no, don't say that,' Josie interrupted, 'just tell her I was a bit kind.'

Auntie Varley, pouring a drop more gin into Auntie Beattie's mug, looked as if she didn't know what either of them were talking about. But Josie knew it wouldn't do her any harm when Ivy was told she'd been helpful to Auntie Beattie Bassey. Pleasing the dressmaker was a feather in her cap, which as time went on might get a nice dress or two for Ivy; and as far as Josie Turner was concerned, a nod was as good as wink to a blind horse.

Persistent bombing to the west of Hermitage Quays had somehow left St Paul's Cathedral still standing, but early the next week a direct hit badly damaged St Patrick's Catholic Church. From the roof of Wilson's Wharf Sonny Bailey saw the bomb explode and shouted it down. 'A big un! All crews, I reckon! Be stuff we can do!'

'Everyone!' Josie commanded. 'All of you! Over St Patrick's!' She pointed her iron bar and led the way. The fire brigade wouldn't get there straight away so the Dead End Kids needed to be quick.

The bomb had hit the nave of the church near the entrance. It was all toppled pillars and heaps of rubble, with fallen roof beams blazing up in smoke; but the crypt had been closed down as a shelter so no lives were at risk – except Father Wearden's, who was coughing violently into a scarf.

Josie took it all in, the height of the blaze and their paltry buckets of water. 'Dougie and Ray, get off with your crews. Get back for another shout. This is miles too big for us.'

Jimmy was skirting the fire and helping the priest to the apse end of the church. He stood the old man by the altar to lean and fight for air, and after he'd found enough of it the priest coughed out a few words to him as he was helped into the open.

'I'm seeing to Father,' Jimmy shouted back to Josie.

Josie ordered the rest of her crew to tackle the edges of the blaze where a few pews might be saved. 'Not a lot we can do.' And she was relieved to hear a fire engine pull up outside. 'We're off. Jimmy, you follow us back.'

'I will, sure, but the oul lad's in bad need of an ambulance...'

Josie ran out as hoses were being unrolled to a hydrant.

The Leading Fireman gave her a thumbs-up.

'Over to you, mate,' she told him. She was going to say more but there was Liz the motorbike messenger skidding up behind the fire engine. 'Ambulance!' Josie told her. 'Father Wearden's down the other end, smoked like a kipper.'

Liz looked to the fireman for permission and got a thumbs-up. She pulled up her machine to race back to HQ, waving at Josie. 'Keep on keeping on, lassie.'

'Will do.' And as she said it Josie couldn't help but point her iron bar towards Wilson's Wharf, leading the way back to base.

By the time the ambulance arrived Father Wearden was in a really bad way. Jimmy had laid him on the grass between two gravestones, resting his head on a folded coat.

'Holy Mother of God!' Ambulance-woman Rosie O'Connor bent to the priest who was struggling to breathe, his chest arching and falling. 'Oxygen!' Her number two ran back to the ambulance to fetch it. 'We'll get you to the infirmary, Father.' She looked across the priest at Jimmy, 'He's not breathing so well but oxygen will help.'

'Sure.' They knew each other. Rosie O'Connor was a member of the Catholic congregation. They both crossed themselves. The oxygen cylinder was brought and Jimmy lifted Father Wearden's head for the mask to be fitted over his face.

'Deep breaths. Lie still for a few minutes, Father. In, out, in, out...' Rosie looked up. 'Get the stretcher, Pam. Poor Father. We'll move him directly, after he's got some pure air inside him.'

Jimmy stayed cradling the priest's head while Rosie took a look through the blasted-out windows into the apse. Father Wearden was breathing more steadily now, the hiss of the oxygen taking over from the sound of his wheezing. Pam came with the stretcher.

'I'll get back to my crew...' Jimmy gently lifted the old man's head, helping the others move him onto the stretcher. 'God bless you, Father.' He made his way towards the street with his rolled coat under his arm, running under the bombs, his eyes to the sky like always.

Pam tucked a blanket around the priest and started to strap him to the stretcher while Rosie went closer to the smashed stained-glass window. She shouted through it to the firemen down the church. 'We're away now with Father.' But instead of making off she stopped and stared and took a sharp breath. 'Will you look at this?'

'Look at what?' The Leading Fireman turned from directing his men.

'The candlesticks...'

'I see them.'

'But what can't you see?'

The fireman came to the altar. 'What am I looking for?'

Rosie pointed at the two candlesticks lying on their sides – and at the empty space between them. 'The crucifix. It's always here, Mass or not. Father's firm as a rock about it: Jesus has to be with us always. And it's gone. It's been taken…'

'I don't know anything about that. My men are all with me, down there.' He looked insulted. 'You're not saying…?'

'Of course I'm not saying. But if the candles are here, where's the crucifix?'

They looked all around, under and beyond the altar, through glass, lead, rubble and dust; in the nave and in the vestry; but the crucifix was nowhere to be seen.

'He might've changed his mind. Taken it home to the presbytery. Ask him.'

Rosie went to the stretcher and bent to Father Wearden, but he was breathing noisily in and out – deeply asleep. 'I will when I can. Ready, Pam? Up.' They lifted the stretcher and made their way through the gravestones; but as they came to the ambulance Rosie's sharp eyes were up and down the street, where, in one direction or the other, Jimmy Riley would have gone.

Eileen Riley rented the ground floor of Thirteen Edison Street. She slept in the front room with the girls while the back room was shared by Jimmy and his two younger brothers. They were all asleep when the knock came at the door: more than a knock, a rapping that couldn't be shuffled off by turning over in bed. She put on her raincoat and answered it, to see a policeman – steel helmet, high collar, buttons shining from top to bottom of his tunic; as alert at dawn as she was worn out.

'Oh, no!' Her eyes went to his hands. Was he carrying a telegram?

They were empty. 'Can I come in?'

She stood aside, led him along the passage to the kitchen, where he wouldn't sit, nor would he have a cup of tea.

'Is Jimmy at home, Mrs Riley?'

'He is. And worn out all right, with his frightened horses and his fire duties…'

'And the rest! Do you know where he was during the raid?'

'I do, and he was a blessing to poor Father. He was at St Patrick's helping with the oul soul, and doing his bidding.'

'His bidding?'

From the back bedroom Jimmy heard a man's voice. He slid out of the bed and pulled on a shirt and trousers over his vest and pants, pushed his feet into his boots.

'What is it?' young Liam wanted to know.

'A man in the kitchen, come in the middle of the night!'

'What for? Not about my dada?'

'That's what I want to know.' Jimmy went to the door, but as he put his hand on the doorknob it was already twisting. It opened, and a policeman was standing there, the man from before. 'Hello, Constable, it's yourself, is it?'

'Up and about, are we?'

'More down and out's the fact of it.'

The policeman came straight to the point. 'A Fire Brigade report says there's an item missing from St Patrick's Church. A silver crucifix. It says your fire gang was there tonight.' He stared at Jimmy. 'Up to our old tricks, are we?'

'What old tricks? Nothing's missing, Constable.' Eileen was in the passage, trying to get through. 'The altar crucifix is here with us, for safekeeping.'

'Oh, safekeeping, is it? And who says so, this harum-scarum?' The policeman hadn't taken his eyes off Jimmy.

'Father told Jimmy he was to protect it.'

'Ah. Well, that's Jimmy's tale, and it would be, wouldn't it?'

Jimmy was reaching under the bed. 'You can check with Father.' He pulled out something wrapped in a shawl. 'Here's your crucifix. You can have it if you lock it up safe.'

The policeman stretched his neck inside his high collar. 'No, son. It won't be the crucifix we lock up safe – it'll be you, till we get chapter and verse off your priest...' He reached down to the handcuffs on his belt. 'You've got a track record, my son.'

'Take your hands off my boy!'

'Father can prove it! Father can prove it!'

With a jangle the policeman unhitched the handcuffs – but Jimmy wasn't offering up his wrists. In a sudden twist he leapt for the bed, crawled over Liam, threw up the sash window, and was through it before the boy could stand up and baulk the policeman.

'I'm not stewing in the jug!'

He ran across the back yard, pushed at the gate, and before the policeman could get out through the scullery door he was pelting down the alley towards King Henry's Wharf and the street that led to the infirmary. A whistle blew behind him as he skirted an ARP post and ran, and ran – mouthing one name over and over as he went.

'Father – Father – Father' – until in the end his breath gave out.

# 13

Jimmy came at St Mary's Infirmary from the rear by the nurses' home. He ran round to the entrance, through the gate, and into the vestibule. This was always a busy place whether daylight bright or blackout dim. In here somewhere was Father Wearden, who could clear Jimmy with the truth of things: who could tell the world that he had not stolen the silver altar crucifix, nor ever would.

Dawn or not, the hallway was busy. A stretcher case was being taken into the lift, a trolley pulled by two nurses was heading to the operating theatre, clusters of relatives were standing pulling at their faces, and two young men with 'student' armbands were walking a pregnant woman towards the main door. Jimmy looked up at the list of wards on a sign above the desk. 'FAITH', 'HOPE', 'CHARITY', 'COURAGE', 'NIGHTINGALE'. Beneath them was a harassed-looking sister. He ran over to her.

'I'm looking to see Father Wearden. From St Patrick's. I've got to talk to him. It's almighty important…'

But this woman seemed more Despair than Hope, more a crow than a nightingale; there was no lightness in her voice. 'Visiting hours are from six to eight in the evening. Strictly.'

'I'm from his church, I kept him going till the ambulance came, but I've got to speak with the man…' Jimmy's voice wheedled, and he lowered his head submissively so she would take pity. 'He's my priest…'

'We're here for people's bodies not their souls, young man. If it's urgent that you see him you'll need a policeman or a warden to vouch for you. I'm busy finding beds for casualties, so you come back at six p.m.'

Jimmy seemed to let his body sag. 'Oh. Fair do's. If that's the tune of it…' He backed away, took a few steps towards the main door – but suddenly went the other way and walked fast for the stairs. Up here were Faith, Hope, Charity, Courage and Nightingale.

He was seen. *'Come back!* Nurse! Porter! Mr Leggatt, stop that boy!'

But Mr Leggatt had a limp, took time to get into a rhythm, and it was an army medical orderly who gave faster chase.

A few vital yards ahead of him on the first landing, Jimmy banged open the door of Faith as if he'd gone inside, but ran up another flight towards Hope and then further up to Courage, which was on the top floor. Here the large ward was divided into two. He stopped behind a buttress to get his breath back. A six-foot partition separated the two halves of the ward, and even in the dim lighting it was clear that there were men patients on the left of the divide and women on the right. In this men's section a dozen beds were set along each side of the ward with tables and extra beds down the middle. A sister sat at a desk near the doorway, writing on a chart by the light of a hurricane lamp.

'Will you excuse me, please, Sister, but I've been sent up to see Father Wearden from St Patrick's. He was brought in tonight. I'm not sure if it's this ward or another…'

The sister looked up from her chart, unsmiling. 'Are you a relative?'

'I work for Father in the church. I'm not a relative but he calls me his right arm.' He showed her the cross around his neck. 'It's just I have to speak to him, most urgent, Sister.'

The sister might have been Catholic, too, because she looked at him kindly and gave him an answer – but it was a terrible thing to hear.

'Father Wearden was brought here from Emergency but I'm afraid he passed over half an hour ago. He never regained consciousness. His body's being attended to even now.' She looked down the ward and pointed to where the screens were around a bed at the far end.

'You're sure?'

'Yes, I'm sure.'

'That it's definitely Father?'

She stared up at him. 'Father Seamus Wearden.'

He bowed his head. 'Father, Father, Father,' he said,

hitting his arms helplessly against his side. 'That's a brutal thing – God rest his soul.'

But he could say nothing more because from the top of the stairs the quiet was interrupted by the sounds of scuffing shoes, and through the glass of the door loomed a face. Jimmy took off as the orderly came into the ward. He sprinted down the line of beds, swinging a chair across after him, then pulling a table into the man's path, and suddenly going for the space between two beds, where, with a leap like mounting Topper, he grasped the top of the partition and pulled himself over onto the women's side.

There were screams and shouts as he side-stepped a nurse and ran along the ward back towards the stairs, just beating the orderly to it and charging down to the hallway – to zig-zag through all the comings and goings and run through the exit and into the street…chasing off into the night, with absolutely nowhere to go.

Josie heard the news of Father Wearden and of Jimmy. She went to the stables, she went to the bombed-out church, she went to St Mary's Infirmary, but Jimmy was nowhere to be found. Word was – spread about by the police – that he'd looted a silver crucifix from St Patrick's Church, and when about to be arrested had trampled over his brother and escaped through a bedroom window.

PC Devonshire was saying it all over Hermitage

Quays: 'You tell me, how innocent is a light-fingered Irish boy who'll dive through a window to get away?'

And old George Knight wasn't any comfort. He told Josie he'd seen a sign somewhere saying that looters could be executed. 'I'd run myself. Get strung up for a piece of silver plate? No, thank you, girl!'

Eileen Riley was no help, either, she was scrawny with worry. 'He's a top lad, a fine son,' was all she could say, 'seen us through up to now. Mother Mary look after him.'

Josie had got to find Jimmy. He needed her; the police would be watching his house and there was no Father Wearden to give him protection. Who else could help him sort himself out? She searched the riverside, in and out of the inlets, along the spits of sand and mud where she'd gone looking for Len; under the sea wall, up and down the Stairs. She walked around the Western Dock for any sign of someone skulking who might try to jump a ship. She went up one street and down the next, eyed boarded-up houses, looked down dug-up gas mains, and lingered at Bestward's flattened brewery by saluting a soldier guarding a crater across from a damaged corner house in Marsh Street. The site was cordoned-off with a UXB sign prominent in the middle. If the soldier had been here a while he might have seen something of Jimmy.

'UXB – that's an unexploded bomb.'

The soldier decided he'd talk to this young lady. 'Two bombs come down but only one went bang – the one that caught the house at the other end of the street.' Josie took a step back and looked along the row of houses. She knew what had happened, it was common in streets like this. The shock wave from the bomb had run along the row and given this other end house a good push, like those toyshop ball bearings on strings.

'But the other bomb's under here – so you keep clear, sweetheart.'

'Is it ticking?'

'Not as loud as my heart.'

'Then hang onto your tin hat, soldier, for putting your bits an' pieces in when the blighter goes up.'

'Very funny.'

'All been quiet otherwise? Anyone about much? You 'aven't seen a boy I know, looking for his cat?'

The soldier shook his head. 'Like a graveyard – and I tell you, that house is dead spooky, which don't help. All killed: mother, father, little girl, sitting there looking as if nothing had touched them.'

Josie shivered. The damaged building had a lean on it like a haunted house at a fair. 'See what you mean.'

'Won't catch me going in there, 'less I'm ordered.'

And suddenly the inkling of an idea came into her mind.

'Ta-ta, soldier boy. Don't worry – there ain't no such

things as ghosts.' And she ran off as if she didn't know which way to go. But she did – because, looking at the lean of that house, she'd just had a mad idea about where Jimmy Riley might be.

He was there: where she thought, at the Hermit Hole, reluctant to come out or even to call back when she shouted down. So she went in.

He was crouching behind the oil drum.

'Jimmy, come out from there, you silly devil. I shouted down, it's me, an' only me. I wouldn't stitch you up, would I?'

His head came round the oil drum. He looked terrible. His bright eyes were half closed and his jaw had no jut in it. This wasn't the real Jimmy Riley, it was a bad-dream version.

'I've heard all about it. They're putting it around that you took a silver crucifix an' hid it under your bed…'

'On Father's say-so. He told me. Wanted it kept safe.' Jimmy's voice wasn't his, either; it didn't even sound Irish, more like a whipped cockney kid. 'But I can never prove it now. He died, didn't come back to us again.'

'I know.' Josie went all matter-of-fact, because that's what Ivy would do. If anyone felt sorry for themselves she reckoned one was enough. 'What about the ambulance girls? They say anything?'

'Nothing special. He went to sleep too quick…'

Josie pulled up a broken chair and an old stool. 'Come right out an' talk to me proper.'

Slowly, Jimmy sat on the stool.

'So let's get it straight. No one knows he told you to look after the cross?'

Jimmy shook his head. 'That was before the ambulance came, just after we got there. By the altar in the ruins.'

'I remember seeing you with him...'

'When Rosie came with her ambulance his breathing got better at first, then he drifted off to sleep, an' the sister at St Mary's says he never woke up.'

'You went there, up the infirmary?'

'Sure I did. That's why I ran off. That copper had got his handcuffs out. I couldn't have stood up for myself from inside the lock-up, could I? And how long before they shifted themselves to go and talk to Father?'

He was starting to sound a bit more his old self again. But he was in a tight corner, that was for sure. Without the Father's word he was guilty to the police, and it would be a tough time in an English cell for an Irish looter. She leant forward, looked into the eyes that had lost their twinkle. 'So what've you got in your head, Jimmy? What's your plan for what to do? You can't go home, you can't go to work, an' you can't hide in here for ever...' It was all a downer, but she said it straight, kept her voice loud and clear; things had got to be faced square on.

'It's the oul country, isn't it? I've got to get to Kilmanagh, back to my grandada and the boys and the horses; I'll be looked after there all right...'

Josie said nothing to that. If he went, would he ever come back? The thought gave her a nasty twist in the stomach.

'There's a ship in the Western. The *Gaelic Queen*, waiting to get off.' Jimmy stood up, walked around the barge, briskly now. 'We're neutral, the Irish, and the oul flags are flying on her. She's only waiting for the paperwork. I'll get onto her, an' spin a yarn when they find me—'

'Or tell them the truth and shame the devil.' She heard herself sounding like Ivy.

'Could be. We'll see. When I'm face to face I'll know what tack to take. Anyhow, the big thing's finding out about the going of her.'

'And not getting caught before you do.' But now Josie knew how she could help. 'I'll hang around the dock and chat up an Irish seaman, see what's what – while you keep yourself out of sight.'

Jimmy stopped his walking around. 'An' how easy's that goin' to be? They'll be looking in corners like this all over the quays...'

Josie shook her head. 'Not if I drop a few rumours around that you've cleared off up north – Blackpool. Yorkshire. Scotland.'

'Yeah, but it could be a week or more 'fore she sails, she's only just unloading. An' there's no back door out of here.' He blew out his cheeks. 'Mother Mary, I'm hungry enough right this minute…'

Josie smiled; but it wasn't forced, it came onto her face as a crazy idea suddenly hit her: definitely mad, but if it came off no one would guess where he was.

He stared at her and frowned.

'Grub first,' she said, 'an' different clothes off my dad. You've gotta take a chance on staying here till dark – but that police creep won't be on duty all last night *and* today, and he's your main worry. Then, Jimmy Riley, I've got a daft idea for where you can keep cavy…'

He came and stood by her, squeezed her face gently between his fingers and thumb, put his head on one side. 'So where is this place? Are you magic, Josie Turner…?' His voice was as soft as Irish rain.

'I'm not far short.' She stood up. 'Now I'm off for food an' clobber – an' when I've gone, give that hatch a good turn till it jams. No one can't get in, then, not without a tin opener. But listen out for me when I knock. It'll be the same as the six o'clock news. *Bong, bong, bong – bong.*' She did the London signal from the wireless and went for the ladder with purpose, but for him, not for her – because she didn't want to leave him, and the truth of it was that her mad plan would lead to the last thing she wanted in the world, making sure that she never saw Jimmy Riley again. And that prospect deprived her voice of getting out a 'See you!' as she lifted the Hermit Hole hatch.

# 14

It was another bad night for the East End with devastating damage in the streets and in the docks. Lives were lost, homes flattened, ships sunk, oil tanks set blazing with heat fierce enough to take the skin off firemen's faces. Bombs fractured gas and water mains, cut electricity cables, pulled down telephone wires and ripped up tramlines. The hold of a ship in the Eastern Dock bellowed like a dragon, melting firemen's boots as they tried to stay close enough to keep their hoses on it, until the blast from a high explosive behind them sent an AFS man flying to his death in the flames. Through it all, keeping going on canteen soup, the civil services fought to rescue people and preserve property and goods.

And it was a busy night for the Dead End Kids. Josie sent crews to a road accident at the eastern entrance to the Basin, where Ray Gull put a tourniquet on a Royal Engineers driver; to an incendiary down a cellar where Tony Milner rescued a cat with five kittens; and Josie went with her own crew to a loud shout from Sonny Bailey when a row of PLA houses along Ruby Way took a hit from a landmine.

'Come on, it's a big one!'

This call-out was some way off, as far as they'd ever gone, and when they got there two fire brigade pumps were already fighting fires on either side of three flattened houses. Above them the bombers droned and fighters buzzed; from down on the ground ack-ack guns fired up to where searchlights tried to pinpoint planes; while in the street the fire pumps surged and revved – everywhere noise and clamour. But in all that noise Josie could just hear voices from behind the demolished middle house – and it sounded like trouble back there. Running around the fire engines she took her crew to where a heap of rubble lay across an Anderson shelter, with people pulling at bricks and slates, joists and slats. 'We've got to get 'em out before they suffocate!'

A spark from a burning house went down Josie's neck. 'Ouch! You little bugger!' Arthur slapped her back and she went on digging with the others, heaving brick, soil and sand until after twenty minutes a hole was made big enough for them to see hands, then arms, then faces, and eventually the family came crawling out – a middle-aged woman, two crying children and a gran.

There were kisses and 'thank you's, and devastated looks at the demolished houses. Josie stared at the four of them. Their world had been turned upside down and there was nothing much anyone could say to them. But the gran found words. She reached down into her handbag, put her teeth into her mouth, and waved an arm at the remains of their house.

'Well, that wasn't a nice thing to do, was it?'

There was a relieved laugh as blankets came and others took over. At least these people were alive and kicking.

'Job done!' Josie told her crew. But now she'd got another job to do. 'You others get back. Carry on. I've got a bit of business to see to.' Her stare and her voice brooked no questions.

'OK, Jose.' Arthur pulled the box-cart down the road and Josie followed them a short way before taking a different turning, heading towards Old Salt Creek and the Hermit Hole.

During the day she'd fed Jimmy and kitted him out from her dad's cupboard. She'd found a shirt, an old cap, and a threadbare three-quarter coat that had been going to the dustmen. These nights were getting chilly, and she shivered as she banged the signal on the side of the barge. The hatch was opened quickly.

'Come on out, Jimmy, put your cap on an' pull it down tight.'

'Tight? The devil's miles too big for my little head.'

'All the better for hiding your face. You can stuff it out when we get where we're going.'

'Which is where, tell me?' Jimmy fell in beside her as she half-walked, half-ran in the direction of St Mary's. 'Not the infirmary…?'

'No – past it. Come on.'

The police were out in force – at incidents, outside

shelters, directing traffic, and seeing to people in a panic – definitely too busy to be trawling a dragnet for a young Irish looter. All the same, Josie kept her eyes skinned. It was getting near the sort of time when the raids usually ended, and tonight she'd like things to go on longer. People had their minds full when bombs were coming down.

As fast as she could she took Jimmy to the house with the tottering wall near the UXB site. A line of red paraffin lights marked where the shoring-up timbers were sticking into the road. 'Hold back.' Josie peered around the corner but couldn't see anyone guarding anything. Had the Bomb Disposal boys been and the soldier gone? Was this such a good hiding place any more?

But what was that? Over on the far side of the site she'd seen the quick flash of a face; someone lighting a fag. 'Stay here!' Pushing Jimmy behind the timbers she crept forward until she could crouch on the pavement and stare. And by a sudden light in the sky she saw him: a soldier, not as tall as the other one, but definitely a soldier in a tin hat, sheltering under the archway of the brewery. She doubled back to Jimmy. 'Soldier-boy's over there, under the arch. Get in the porch.'

The door of the house was nailed shut with a couple of planks, but using her iron bar they prised them apart and pushed at the door, which gave. She fished out her torch, and shining it around, she could see what had happened. When the blast had hit the house all the ceilings had come down. There'd been no fire, there was no smell of smoke, nor of gas; but bricks, plaster, rafters, dust and slates covered everything. Looking up the stairs she could see searchlights through a hole in the roof; but there was no getting to the landing because the stairs were matchwood, worse than Auntie Beattie Bassey's that time. In the back room there was furniture under the debris: a table, chairs, a settee. The windows were boarded over, and so were the window and door of the kitchen, where the bath from upstairs was half hanging down the wall. And beyond the back door was…what? Probably a scullery or an outhouse, but Josie didn't bother with that. She stood, looked around her, and had a think. The front door had been nailed up and the front wall supported by timbers, so Civil Defence had done all they wanted to do for now. And from what the first soldier had said, there wouldn't be any family coming here any time soon. Plus, the two of them had got in here without being seen, so no one knew they were here, and Jimmy wouldn't have to be out on the streets while he waited for his ship to sail. Just what she'd hoped for.

'Here you are. Your hidey-hole. No one won't bother you here.'

'Clever. But what's the soldier for?' Jimmy lifted his cap to scratch his head. 'Do soldier boys guard damaged houses?'

'No. He's guarding something else.'

'What, then? The old brewery? A few broken bottles?'

'No.' Josie counted to five. 'He's guarding a bomb. A dud, I reckon.' She'd got to tell him, it wouldn't be fair otherwise.

'*A bomb?* What sort?'

'One o' them that goes bang. Except, I don't think it will. Time bombs don't have long fuses, do they? If that thing out there was going up it would've done it by now.'

'Till another bomb comes down and gives the devil a good shaking…'

'Never! Two dropping that close together? What are the chances of that?'

'Well, we shall see, shan't we?' But now he changed his tone, started speaking slower, softer. 'But, thanks for doing this, Jose. I'll wait for a crack of light an' clear myself a bit of space in the back room there.' He went to the cold tap and turned it. It worked, rusty at first, but it worked. 'I've got a drink, an' I kept back some bread.' He patted his coat pocket. 'Thanks to you I'm all set up a treat.'

'I'll bring some more grub soon.'

'Josie, you're a real oul doll…' His voice was in his throat as he stood very close to her, she could feel the warmth off him from their running. He put his hands on her shoulders, firm and steady. In the darkness the peak of his cap touched her forehead. His eyes looked into hers, not blinking. She held her breath.

And the All Clear sounded.

'I've gotta go. My mum'll go bananas if she thinks I've gone missing…'

He stood back. ''Course.'

'I'll pull the wood back over the front door – an' I'll see you tomorrow – after I've had a chat with a bloke off the *Gaelic*.'

'God bless you.'

The special moment had passed, and it was almost a handshake goodbye as they touched on her way out.

'See you, Jimmy.'

'Sure, see you, Jose.' And he let her out under the porch.

The soldier was nowhere to be seen, and Josie ran back to Wilson's Wharf as quickly as she could. And thank God she'd beaten Ivy back from her concert party. Auntie Varley was looking around among the stragglers so she pretended to come out from behind the lavatory curtain.

'Sorry about that. But when you gotta go, you gotta go!'

And in a different sense, she reckoned sadly, that went for Jimmy Riley, too. Which had to be the reason for the new, strange pain she felt inside her.

# 15

Rotten news lay on Josie's doormat. Not terrible news like something about her dad but a letter from the London County Council Schools' Department. Whenever the letterbox rattled, Ivy would rush to the door, even though the worst news would come with a knock and a telegram handed over. This letter, though, was addressed to Mr and Mrs S. Turner, and when she read it Ivy put a satisfied look on her face as if she'd just been sent a rent rebate.

'You're back to school, Monday, my girl.'

'Sugar!'

'Come on, you can't moan, you've had a good run. But it's not back to Stepney Street, that's still a fire station.'

'Where, then?'

'Addison Road.'

'That's bloomin' miles away!' And it was a school well known for being strict; Shirley's mother had transferred Shirley out of there, even when they lived in the same road. Stepney Street had a soft old headmaster, Mr Winters, but he'd been evacuated with the school, while over at Addison Road there was a headmaster called Mr White who caned girls as well as boys. Josie knew darned well the two of them wouldn't get on, although if he tried to lay a hand on her she'd flatten him. Thank God it would only be till she left at Christmas.

'So you'd better start sorting yourself out…'

Josie looked down at her clothes. She was in her daytime frock and cardigan and her street shoes, so there wasn't much sorting to do, this was what she'd wear to school.

'Sort yourself in your head, girl. Up here. Hold a pencil in your hand for five minutes. Go over your spellings and your times tables. "Once two is two…"'

Josie snorted. Her dad always recited her tables with her. 'Eleven twelves, what's that, then, *Mother*?'

The two of them swapped cocky looks. 'A hundred and thirty-two, thanks.'

'Anyhow, I'm going out.' Josie stepped over the mat to get to the door – to be stopped by what Ivy said next.

'Not going out after that Jimmy Riley, are you?'

'Who?'

'You know damned well who. I bumped into Eileen Riley up the grocer's. He's gone off somewhere, they say he took something from the church…'

Josie shook her head as if she couldn't make head or tail of what Ivy was saying. 'I don't know nothing about that.' And she got out before the conversation went any further – heading straight for the Western Dock.

So it was all over Hermitage Quays about Jimmy Riley. Which made it all the more urgent to know when the *Gaelic Queen* was shipping out. For Jimmy, that was. Definitely not for her.

It wasn't too hard to find a friendly Irish seaman, but not inside the dock. People couldn't just walk in and out, and the dock walls were high. She loitered on the other side of the road until a group of men came out of the gate, waved through in a cluster by the dock policeman.

'Down one for me, Paddy.'

*Paddy.* They had to be Irish, then. She gave it a few moments and followed them, when one turned around and gave her the eye. She smiled back, but kept a good few yards behind. And soon she knew which pub they were coming to: the London River, the pub she never wanted to see again in her life. They went for the door of the public bar.

'Oi! 'Scuse me, mister…'

The man who'd given her the eye turned back. 'What is it, girl? Not after keeping me from my glass, are you…?'

'I'm not.' She sounded Irish herself. 'I just wanted to know. My sister fancies your Second Mate, or someone…' That sounded roughly right. 'Wants to know when he's sailing so's she can say a proper goodbye.'

The man narrowed his eyes. He was smallish in a high-necked sweater. 'Is that so? It's grief at the parting, is it – not being left with something she doesn't want?' He nodded down at her stomach.

'No. Don't be daft. Nothing like that. She's just…
a bit soft on him, you know…' That was the best she
could do.

'Well, I'll tell you.' He wiped his mouth as if he was
already halfway down that glass. 'Not tomorrer, two
mornings after, that'll be Thursday, we're off on the tide,
around half-eleven.' He pulled a sad face. 'An' us back
aboard by ten the night before.'

'Ah.'

'So tell her to come down here. But this place shuts at
half-nine so not to come late.'

'Yeah. Right. I'll tell her.'

He looked her up and down. 'Fancy a lemonade and
a ginger biscuit?'

'No, thanks. I've gotta do jobs for my mum.'

'Hard luck. Then I'll get to my Guinness.' And with
another wipe of his mouth he went inside.

*Yes!* She'd got what she wanted. But more than that,
she'd got an idea for getting Jimmy into the Western
Dock. When this lot had finished their last drink-up and
went back to their ship, Jimmy could pull down his cap
and slip past the dock police with them. It had all been
very matey at the gate, and dock security was more about
stuff coming out than spies getting in. Then once he was
inside Jimmy could skulk off behind a pile of cargo and
wait for his chance to get aboard the ship. Which

wouldn't be too hard, she reckoned, for a clever boy like him.

The siren had sounded, the shelter was busy, and all the Dead End Kids had turned up ready to do their bit. Now Josie gave Auntie Varley the slip and handed Sonny Bailey the iron bar. 'Do us a favour an' take over.' She put on the look of someone with a sick cat. 'It's Ivy, my mum…'

'She ill?'

'Not sure…' Ivy was singing in shelters over at Mile End that night, and she'd gone to get her bus before the siren went.

'Fair enough.' He smacked the iron bar against the palm of his hand.

'Don't lose it, will you?'

''Course I won't.'

She pulled the same worried face for her crew, mouthing 'My mum'; and with her excuses made she doubled back to her house and picked up her secret supplies: an old box of dates, a bag of broken biscuits, a Fry's peppermint chocolate bar, a small brown loaf and three apples. Her savings had also stretched to a box of Swan Vesta matches, and she'd pinched half a candle from the cupboard under the stairs. She stuffed it all into an old shopping bag and ran off through the air raid to the UXB site. And that wasn't easy. ARP wardens and policemen stopped anyone out and about in the raids, which were good times for looters to do their business, so she had to skulk and crouch, run and freeze, but at last she made it.

A soldier was still there by the brewery archway, moving about a bit more than the last one. The bombers seemed to be hitting further south tonight, going for the other side of the river; but according to Jimmy this bomb here could still go up if the ground shook hard enough. So why hadn't the army seen to it yet? They had to reckon the same as she did – it was a dud.

The trouble was, this soldier was too fidgety to let Josie go for the front door of the house. She was on the other side of the road, and if she crossed over to get near to it he'd see her. So she decided to go the back way. She went along the row of houses and clambered through where the end house had taken a direct hit. Now she was in a line with all the back yards. Carefully – and awkwardly with her shopping bag – she started climbing over the fences along towards the house at the other end. But it was slow going; she had to have her wits about her; she couldn't bank on no one being in their kitchen. At last she crept up to the back of the end house and came to a lean-to porch – which was giving off a strong smell of cats' pee, worse inside than out. Not breathing too deeply she knocked on the door. Rap, rap, rap – *rap*: again the wireless news signal. But Jimmy didn't answer. She did it again; and again, but nothing. Had he gone? Had the soldier found him, captured him, locked him up? Had the roof fallen in on him? She knocked again, louder: thump, thump, thump – *thump*. And still nothing. She put down the shopping bag. Where the devil was he? What had happened to him?

Stupid! Hadn't he said he'd make himself a bit of space in the back room? With planes going over and the ack-ack firing he mightn't have heard her banging in the porch. But it was going to be tricky getting to the back room window. Most of the houses in a terrace had back room windows facing to the back, but being the end house, this back room window was on the side – in full view of the soldier. She left her shopping bag in the smelly porch and went crouching towards the corner of the house. With the light fading fast it was hard to see into the shadows where the soldier was standing so she couldn't take any chances, she had to keep her eyes skinned. Now she thanked God for her slacks because she was crawling like a commando to keep low, over brick and slate and splintery wood until she got herself where she needed to be, lying flat under the window she wanted. Looking across at the archway and seeing no one she reached up and pummelled on the boarding. Forget the wireless signal, she just pummelled. But, nothing. She pummelled again. Still nothing.

Now she did start believing the worst. The council

had come to inspect the house and found him. Or the soldier had decided to see what he could find inside, some fags, some drink, money under a floorboard. Whatever, Jimmy was banged up in a police cell right now, and with Father Wearden in the mortuary there was no one to speak for him. Jimmy Riley was done for.

But not yet. *Think positive.* She hadn't tried the front of the house, had she? He could be waiting for her knock in the hall, the way she'd gone out. She squinted across at the archway. She'd be seen getting round to the front door unless she went on her hands and knees, but she'd done it once…

'Jose!'

She went rigid, lying there.

'Jose!'

She lifted her head, looked behind her. Jimmy was poking his head round the corner at the back. He must have heard her knocking and come out through the kitchen.

'Get back! Soldier!'

His head disappeared and she crawled back the way she'd come, her knees someone else's now – and her slacks, too: she'd have to tell Ivy she'd fallen over in the blackout.

Jimmy was in the back porch. 'Jose! You're a fierce good friend.' He kissed her on the forehead, and pulled her into the house, took her through to the back room.

'Didn't hear you till the last. Come into the parlour.'

'"Said the spider to the fly!"'

She dusted herself down, fetched the shopping bag and dived into it. She lit the candle, sticking it onto the table. Now she could see how he'd cleared the floor and pushed a couch beneath the window, made himself a cosy corner.

'I had a good lie there, listening. An' caught some shut-eye. It's all dead quiet with your man's bomb.'

'An' I'm banking on it staying like that, till Thursday night…'

'Is that the sailing? What's the craic?' He was restless, but his voice was calm; still Jimmy Riley's.

'Hang on.' She handed him an apple and tore off a corner of the loaf. 'Get that inside you.'

He did. He found two chairs and pulled them up to the table. 'You're a champeen, Josie Turner.'

She told him what she'd found out about the sailing time, and her idea for getting into the dock. 'It's all matey at the gate, just squeeze yourself in at the back, the Irish won't know you're not off another boat, and the police won't know you're not one of them.'

He ate and nodded. 'Play both sides against the middle. Sounds all right. Just the ticket.' He looked at her through the flicker of candlelight.

'Hope so.' But was this the last she'd see of him? Was this the look she'd have to remember for always, this

Jimmy Riley, his eyes not blinking as he looked at her?

'Here y'are.' He bit off a fleshy piece of apple and offered it to her – which she took, not for any hunger but for the sharing.

'I've got another smidge of a favour, Jose – if you can do it for us.'

''Course. What?' If it was in her power she'd do anything for this boy.

'Fetch us another gansey, if you can. I don't know where I'll be holed up on the ship, but it can get perishing at sea. The wind cuts like a crocked bottle.'

She angled her head, his way. 'A *gansey*?'

'A jumper, a sweater, that sort of thing. Drop back tomorrow wi' something, if you can.'

She leant towards him, feeling the warmth off the candle on her face. 'I will. It'll be easier in the day with other people cutting through to the shops. I can stroll past a couple of times till I get the chance to knock. At the front.'

'I'll listen out. Also at the front.' He smiled at her.

Her hand went to the shopping bag. 'Want a Fry's bar?'

'I'll save it. An' we won't use too much of this candle, don't know where I'll find myself on the *Gaelic*.'

'No.'

They both went quiet. Josie looked around at the dark corners of the room, came back to the candle that was holding her and Jimmy in its circle of light. 'You know what?' she said.

'What?' His eyes were wide, and greeny-blue.

'Be a nice little place this. For anyone. Somewhere like this, without a war on.'

'It would.' He stretched out his hand and laid it on her palm, the sudden touch of it feeling very special. 'Be like playing mamas an' dadas.'

Her throat went tight. 'Would be a bit.' She straightened her back and took her hand from under his. 'You sure you don't want that Fry's bar?'

He laughed. 'No, I'll save it. All sweet things are worth waiting for.'

She nodded. They were, if anyone could be sure they'd ever happen. But in a war where ships were being bombed and people were hundreds of miles apart, no one could ever get too hopeful.

She looked him in the eyes and stared him out. 'We'll have to see how things go, won't we, Jimmy?'

# 16

Fire and Ambulance shared Stepney Street School. Each had its own senior officers and its own bungalow building, the playground was divided between ambulances and fire engines, while common ground was the social life of the off-duty men and women. At some stage in its history the school had built a corrugated classroom against one of the buildings, with 'Deaf Girls' painted over its door. This was now a sort of social club with a bar, a dartboard and a piano, a popular place with both fire and ambulance people after the All Clears had sounded.

It was in the early hours when Liz McKenzie carried a small glass of Bell's from the bar and looked for a seat somewhere, the place full of unbuttoned uniforms, grimy faces and quiet conversation. There was a spare place at a card table where two ambulance-women were talking over gin and tonics.

'Is this seat free, ladies?'

'Sit you down.'

'Liz, isn't it?'

'McKenzie.' Liz looked tired, took a first sip of her Scotch.

'Rosie and Pam.' The three of them fluttered their free hands.

'Don't let me interrupt…'

'Oh, it's not a lot. I'll finish fast. I belong to St Patrick's, and off-duty I'm helping set up the church hall for worship…'

Liz took another decent-sized sip, eyes rather glazed.

'I'm telling Pam here one of our church boys has gone missing, been accused of stealing the crucifix from the altar…'

'Aye, there's a lot of that goes on.'

'Which is a travesty of justice, because the boy's innocent. He never stole a thing. Sometimes they're very quick to jump, the police.'

Liz nodded, absently.

'If only they'd asked us. We attended the incident, looked to Father Wearden, my priest. He died, sadly, but he came to in the ambulance enough to tell us the crucifix was in good hands…'

'A relief, then.' Liz stifled a yawn.

'In young Jimmy's hands, the boy who's gone missing.'

'That's a vindication for the lad.'

'Except he's still on the run, that's what I'm telling Pam, he doesn't know what Father said. And he's a decent lad. One of those Dead End Kids with their stirrup pumps and sand. Works at the stables.'

Liz put down her glass. More focussed now. 'I know the Dead End Kids. They saved the wooden bridge.'

'Well, if any of them knows where Jimmy is, his

mother doesn't. Poor soul's going desperate worrying about him.'

Liz got up. 'Well, I'm for my cot. But if I see them – and I sometimes do – I'll tell them what you said.'

'Tell them Jimmy's in the clear and he can show himself again. We'll vouch for that.'

'I will. And I'll bid you goodnight, then.' Liz squeezed her way out of the Social Club and went over to the women's dormitory in the fire brigade building – where she was asleep in her uniform within ten minutes.

Now Josie would be in real trouble. She wasn't going to touch Len's sweaters because she didn't want to see anyone wearing one of them, so the sweater she was taking was one of her dad's, good and thick, his favourite for going out on the river. She'd have to have some excuse before he ever came home on leave; but she'd think of something when the time came, she usually did.

The hot summer was well over, it was overcast and threatening rain, and next week was back to school, but the black cloud hanging over her was the thought of saying goodbye to Jimmy Riley. She had a twist in her stomach she couldn't get rid of, whatever she did.

There was no sign of a soldier as she came to the house, although everything else seemed the same – the cordon was still up and there were no Bomb Disposal people on the site. She could knock on the door now if she was quick.

'Wotcha Jose!'

She spun round.

'Josie! Over here!' There on the other side of the street was Shirley Farmer and her mother, both in loose headscarves, no doubt just come from Madame de Marne's up by the station.

'Oh, wotcha Shirl. Had your hair done?'

'A Veronica Lake. What you doing here?'

'Not a lot.'

Mrs Farmer pulled Shirley's arm. 'Well, don't do it too hard. Come on, Shirley, I need to get home…'

Josie stood and watched them go; a mistake, because Shirley looked round and saw that she hadn't moved, for all the world as if she was up to something. Josie turned quickly and walked up towards the station, the twist in her stomach beginning to turn into a proper pain, like something serious.

That morning Liz McKenzie was on a routine message run, a quick turn-around of the Blue Dispatch Watch. She was taking incident reports from Stepney Street to District Control, and with closed roads and diversions her quickest way was along by the river. The streets were clearer here and she could put some speed on; but she slowed down as she rode past Wilson's Wharf stables where a stable-girl was mucking out onto a cart. She pulled over and sat straddling her bike.

'Yes?' The girl looked on edge. 'You police?'

'No, fire brigade. It's about Jimmy. I heard something he'll be pleased to know about.'

The girl still looked cautious. 'Well, he ain't here.'

'It's something very good.'

'He still ain't here. What is it, anyhow?'

'I'm sure you'll know about his fix – about what they're saying about him…'

'Could do.'

'Well, he's done nothing wrong. Two of our ambulance-women can vouch for it. The priest asked him to do what he did.'

'I can't tell him nothing, he's not hiding here.'

'So you said.' Liz patted her dispatch pouch. 'I'll have to get on. But if you do hear word of him…'

The girl started raking again. 'I'd be the last to know anything. He's not sweet on me. If anyone can tell you the ins and outs of Jimmy Riley it's a girl called Josie Turner.'

'Oh, I know Josie. Thanks, anyway. But if you should –'

'Hold on!' The girl pointed her broom across the street. 'Over there.' A woman and a girl in loose headscarves were going by. 'That kid'll get a message to Turner, they're all in the same soppy gang.'

'Thank you.' Liz got off her bike and crossed the street. 'Excuse me…'

The pair stopped. She spoke to the girl. 'I know you, don't I? The wooden bridge?'

The girl went crimson and shook her head. 'Never heard of it.'

'I'm looking for Josie. I've got something I need to tell her.'

'We've just seen her. Up Marsh Street.'

'Marsh Street?'

The woman pulled a face. 'By the old brewery, on the way to the station. Come on, Shirley.' And she walked the girl away.

'Thank you.' Liz kick-started her bike and rode it in that direction, up to the King's Head crossroads – where, instead of turning right towards District Control at Southend Road she turned left past a fallen road sign and on along Marsh Street towards the station.

A heavy lorry piled high with concrete sewer rings was rumbling along ahead of her, and with the shoring-up of a house sticking out into the road it was hard to overtake; but she managed it by mounting the pavement; then she stopped and took a good look around her. Next to the damaged house was an open space beside Bestward's bombed-out brewery, cordoned off and with UXB signs displayed.

'Excuse me,' she shouted to a soldier over by the

brewery archway as she straddled her bike. 'Haven't seen a young lass anywhere here, have you?'

'No, love. Just come on duty.'

Liz looked at her watch. 'Never mind.' The lorry was rumbling close up behind her and she'd have to get out of its way. 'Not to fret. Just a chance.'

But the soldier was paying little attention to her. As the lorry came heavily along the street he started running towards it, waving his arms. 'Oi! You can't come down here! Big stuff's banned! Didn't you read the signs?'

'We've got a bombed sewer to get to!'

Liz started her bike and turned around to go back past the lorry. She'd dallied enough already – and life was too short to fall out with the Chief Fire Officer. She looked ahead, saw her way clear, and twisted her throttle to open up and get on with her job…

Josie was inside the house. She'd waited for her chance, and when the soldier had gone marching off along the pavement, she'd slipped back round the corner to the front door, where Jimmy quickly opened up.

'Hello to you, Jose.'

She went inside and without a by-your-leave pulled her dad's sweater down over Jimmy's head. It was too big, her dad was a bulky man and although Jimmy was tall he was as skinny as a jockey; but the wool was thick and warm, so he'd have to manage somehow.

'Will you look at me in this? Like a ferret in a double bed. There's room for two in here…'

'I'll come in with you, then.' It was a joke, but it didn't get a smile, just a long silence.

They went into the back room where neither of them seemed to know what to say or do. They just stood there, and Josie nearly found herself saying something about the weather. Until—

'I'll tell you something, Josie Turner…' Jimmy ran his fingers through his hair, looked deadly serious, his eyes staring into hers. 'When I get back to the oul country I'll take pen and paper and I'll write to you…'

'That'll be nice.' His voice was soft, and she'd like to listen to it all day. But she couldn't hang about too long. 'Fifteen Monks Street.' Her mouth was almost too dry to say it.

'And when the war's all done with and you're of the age…'

'What about then?'

But he didn't get anything out. Suddenly the boarded-up window came bursting in. The floor rocked beneath their feet, Josie was thrown across the room, Jimmy too, and the whole house shook, the walls loudly cracking, and plaster and laths came crashing down. Above them was the sky as slates fell and bricks split. This place was caving in – on top of them!

'Quick! Out the back!'

They ran through to the kitchen, where the back door was flat on the ground, the house groaning, crumbling, rafters falling and water spraying from the pipework. Running out through the porch they chased across the open space, seconds before the whole building caved in – a thudding collapse, all brick dust and plaster, flapping curtains, feathers, horsehair and flying glass.

Josie could see the bomb crater, three yards across. There was no sign of the soldier but in the road a large lorry was over on its side. And – what was that? – a motorbike half on, half off the pavement, its engine running and someone lying near it, dead still. She ran there, Jimmy tight behind.

'Jeepers!' A quick look told Josie who this was – the AFS dispatch rider, the Scottish girl, Liz. There wasn't much blood on her face, just a small cut on her forehead, but her eyes were staring open and they didn't blink, and her body was twisted like a rag doll's. She was dead. 'Oh my God!'

People were shouting from along the street, running towards them through the brick dust.

'Quick! On the back!' Josie scooped up the girl's cap, crammed it on her head, picked up the motorbike and straddled it. In a shake Jimmy was up behind her. A quick look at the hand grips – the same as on her dad's bike – and she twisted the throttle open and roared them off down Marsh Street – *balance, balance, balance* – off towards Stepney Green, anywhere away from here.

That poor Liz was dead, but Jimmy wasn't going to be a loser, too. No way was he heading for prison – not while Josie Turner was in control of things.

# 17

Josie followed her nose and bits of memory out to Epping Forest. Those motorbike spins up behind her dad were locked in her head, and, somehow, so was the way to get there. Buckhurst Hill; Woodford: she remembered the road signs from those sunny Sundays.

No one stopped them. It had been a good touch, picking up Liz's AFS cap, but she felt sickened to have it. She wanted to wear one of these when she was older, but right now she couldn't get the sight of the poor dead girl out of her head, lying on the bomb site with her hair all unravelled. She shuddered, shook the picture away, and with only a couple of wrong turnings and double-backs, she rode them to the King's Oak pub and the forest cinder track where her dad used to imagine he was a speedway ace.

'Steady on, Jose. You're not on Topper now!'

Jimmy was gripping her tight around the middle and there was some thrill in that, but she had to keep her concentration on steering the bike now it was off the road. She took them deeper into the forest, twisting and turning along a winding track, the trees getting denser and denser to where the light found it hard to reach the ground.

She took a still narrower track – and suddenly

gripped hard on the brakes, throwing Jimmy tight up behind her.

'What a turn-up! Just the job!'

'And me with my back coming through my front!'

'Sorry! But look at that.'

A huge tree had crashed down in a storm, leaving a great bowl of earthy roots sticking into the air, reaching up higher than a man, all overgrown with brambles. It looked like a small leafy cave. A brilliant hideout.

'No one won't find you in there.'

Jimmy seemed torn in two. Yes, he was nodding at the hideout, but then he was turning and twisting his head. 'How the Holy Joe am I going to find my way back for Thursday night?'

'Like me, follow your nose!'

'Follow it where?'

'Back.' She pushed the motorbike among the brambles, pulled at Jimmy's arm and took him under the overhanging roots. 'We had to get well clear. The bomb went off.' She shivered. 'People were coming, so I've got you away and brought you out here, right? Where no one's ever heard of St Patrick's Church or its silver cross.'

'Sure enough. But I'm here, an' the *Gaelic's* there.' He arched an arm upwards as if the ship was on the moon.

'And you're here because if you're still around the quays they'll nab you, ten to one. The coppers'll be keeping watch on your house, and the stables, and they know all the other places to look, like the barge. But out here you've got a good place to kip tonight, an' you can even have a lie-in if you like. Then you start walking. It's easy. Woodford, Buckhurst Hill, more or less one road. No one'll know you. Use your noddle, ask someone, get as far as you can, an' lie low tomorrow night. Wanstead Flats is good, get in one of them trenches they've dug – then Thursday you toddle on for the pub, and wait for the Irish coming out.'

'Sure. A piece of cake!' He lifted his cap and ruffled his hair. 'But if I can get into the dock some other way I will. I'm in and out times enough with the horses…'

'That's the stuff.' Josie put her head on one side, smiled at him. 'Sorry I can't come and pick you up with the bike but I've got to get it back.'

'I know that.' He stood up straighter. 'Jesus, 'course I'll be all right. I'm not some useless bowsie. If I can't feed my face off a market stall and worm my way into the Western I'm not fit to know a sparky girl like you.'

Josie straightened too. That was nice to hear. 'I can't stay here long, Jimmy. If I'm not in for my tea my mum'll go potty. She's off out singing later.'

For a while neither of them spoke. Deep in the forest it was eerily quiet. And then Josie was turned inside out.

'I'll tell you what, Josie Turner…' He came closer.

'What?'

'When all this is over an' done with, an' you're old enough –' he waved his hand at the trees, the sky, the war – 'you can come to the oul country an' we'll jump the broomstick…'

She frowned at him. *Jump the broomstick?* What had a broomstick got to do with anything?

'It's what the tinkers say for joining up…'

*'Joining up?* To what? The Irish army?'

'To each other. Getting hitched, you soft mineral-water. One day.'

His words didn't sink in at first, but as he went on staring at her and he smiled, she froze – a sort of delicious hot freeze she'd never known before.

'An' you'll be my sweetheart till then, Jose, whatever the miles between us…' He put his hands on her shoulders, drew her to him, and kissed her on the mouth. She pulled away in shock, but before she knew it she was kissing him back – fierce and deep and lingering, her eyes closed, her body pressed hard against his. She found she could breathe while they kissed, and they could talk to each other through sounds in their throats.

'I've got to go.' She pulled away. Her mouth was wet, but she wasn't going to wipe it.

'Sure. You've got to go.' He made no bones about it. He was a real Irish gentleman.

'And I'll try to, I'll try like hell, but I might not see you again, Jimmy, unless it's to come an' wave at the

*Gaelic Queen*.' It was a terrible thought, light on the words, heavy in the meaning.

'You won't see me if you do. I'll be deep hidden till she's well out to sea.'

'God bless you, Jimmy Riley.'

'An' God bless you, Josie Turner. Until next time…'

'Yeah. Till then.'

She was both high and low. She was a girl who'd just been properly kissed and also a girl who had to get back home in time for tea. But she was definitely not the girl who'd ridden them there. She pulled the motorbike free of the brambles and kick-started it. And without another word, no looking back, she rode it through the trees towards High Beech and the roads to Hermitage Quays, looking all straight and official in Liz McKenzie's AFS cap but with her feelings all over the place.

As she got nearer to Hermitage Quays she slowed the bike and cruised around a few strangers' streets that weren't too far away for walking home. She turned into a desolate dead-end off Cable Street, which led to a gloomy locked-up scrapyard. There was a sign stuck on the metal gate. 'CALLED UP. ALL ENQUIRIES 18 BELFAST HOUSE'. Beside the gate was a heap of bomb debris and turned-out rubbish. With her eyes all around her, she put the bike half in and half out of the heap. Give it a day to be found, she thought, then if it was still there tomorrow she'd get word to the fire brigade somehow. She'd borrowed the bike, not stolen it, and no way was she going to be an outlaw like Jimmy.

She headed for home thinking no more about it, still filled with the mixed-up thrill of that kiss, and the terrible thought of not seeing her Jimmy again for a long, long, time – perhaps not ever.

And although she didn't have a Royal Artillery sweetheart brooch like Ivy wore, she felt the same as her, someone separated from her man by this rotten war.

The shock of what had happened hit her on the Wednesday. The terror of the war hit home: the UXB explosion, just getting out of that house in time, seeing the dead, twisted, body of Liz the AFS girl, and the real sadness of saying goodbye to Jimmy in Epping Forest. The Dead End Kids were real, too, but suddenly all that seemed more like a dangerous game she was playing. She mooned around the house until Ivy started looking at her with one eye half closed.

'Are you all right, girl? Something going on with you?'

'No.'

'You sure?'

'Sure I'm sure.'

Now Ivy gave her a hard stare. 'Then you can stop being useless and do a bit more for me till school starts on Monday.'

'Like what?'

'Like a bit less mouth and a dose of ironing. Or give the windows a rub. Something useful.'

Josie chose to go to pay the rent instead, and took herself to the river where she sat on the steps of the Captain Lowry Stairs. But today her thoughts weren't on Len but on Jimmy Riley. She pictured every stage of his journey back to Hermitage Quays, nicking an apple from a greengrocer's box, kipping down in a trench on Wanstead Flats, trudging along the streets with his cap pulled down. She saw his pale face, his greeny-blue eyes, and she closed hers to help bring back the special feeling of their kiss. But it had gone; it was a bubble that had burst, and she was left with nothing. Nothing any more.

That night was quiet for the Dead End Kids, the bombing seemed to be upriver, as if Jerry reckoned he'd done for the East End. But the siren had sounded, and the shelter was crowded again – including Jimmy's family.

Josie wasn't sure why Mrs Riley picked her out; surely to God Jimmy hadn't told his mum about her? She came up to Josie at the foot of the steps.

'Have you got any clue, Josie? Have any of you kids heard word about the going of my Jimmy?'

Josie tried to strike the right balance. ''Course, I know he ran off, out of your house…'

'But where to? I've just come from the police station and they've told me...'

'Told you what?'

'They've told me, official. They know he's not guilty. He's in the clear. Rosie from the church has signed a paper saying what Father told her in the ambulance. The boy's as clean as clean – which Father knew, and I know, and he knows himself.'

*Jeepers!* This was fantastic! Brilliant! Jimmy was in the clear! He didn't need to run away to Ireland! She took a quick look upwards. *Oh, thank you, God! Thank you.*

'But he can't know they're not after his tail any more or he'd have come home. I pray to Our Lady he doesn't do some stupid thing. It's driving me skinny till I know he's safe.' Mrs Riley's face came close to Josie's. 'You sure you've no idea where he is?'

Josie put on an empty look while she thought fast. She mustn't let anything slip out just yet. Until that motorbike was safely back with the AFS Mrs Riley mustn't know about her and Jimmy and hiding in the house. They could both be got for taking it, and it was probably as serious as anyone stealing a crucifix. People would definitely have seen the two of them on the motorbike. They could easily pick out her and Jimmy in a line-up. So until it was found, no way could she tell Mrs Riley the truth.

'Search me, Mrs Riley.'

But Mrs Riley was persistent, looked as if she knew more about her and Jimmy than she should. 'You were more a friend of his than most. You do grooming at the stables, don't you?' She was looking as suspicious as Ivy checking the number of fags in her packet of Weights.

Josie shook her head. 'Not a clue. Don't know nothing about where Jimmy's gone, sorry, Mrs Riley.' She suddenly turned to look up the steps. 'Hang on! Gotta go! Someone wants me.'

No one did – and when Mrs Riley looked up, too, it was with a disbelieving face.

Josie went up the steps and listened for a shout – which didn't come. But to get well clear of Mrs Riley she called out Dougie's crew and led them to a false alarm at a shoe shop – feeling in a worse mixed-up state than ever.

It was brilliant that Jimmy was in the clear – but why had she been so stupid, leaving the bike in a back alley? All right, if the fire brigade found it they'd probably forget about it going missing for a few hours, but it would be a different story if it was gone for good. If someone honest handed it in, OK, but what if someone bent had sold it on? They'd soon start taking some serious descriptions of the two who were seen on it.

Why the heck hadn't she done something about it today instead of moping around trying to remember the feel of being kissed? Well, she'd got to sort it tomorrow, top priority, and tomorrow night she'd got to move heaven and earth to make sure Jimmy didn't get anywhere near the *Gaelic Queen*.

# 18

Early that next morning she called for Charlie Drew. It was a clever touch, she thought, choosing him because he wasn't as bright as Arthur but he'd be dead useful if the bike was where she'd left it.

'What you want, Josie?' Charlie was back to school on Monday, too, and he looked as if he'd been making the most of a lie-in.

'Dead End Kids. I might need a hand with something.'

'What?'

'Someone's told me about a scrapyard off Cable Street, bloke's gone in the army or somewhere, they've seen an old motorbike outside…'

'Yeah?'

'Jones's scrapyard might give us something for it, then we can buy some good new rope and stuff…'

Charlie didn't look so sure. 'Why didn't this someone take it there himself?'

'It was an old lady. I know her, she couldn't push a pea off a plate.'

'A motorbike won't have hung around for long…'

'That's what I'm worried about.'

'All right. Give us a minute.'

Charlie went back inside his flat, and Josie waited outside the block. There was still a space in the corridor where a stirrup pump and a red bucket had once been. They weren't hard to have one over, these Jubilee people.

The bike was there! She must have tucked it further behind the rubbish than she remembered. She looked up at the sky and thanked her lucky stars.

'Here, Charlie, look at it.' She started on her spiel. 'This isn't just any old motorbike…'

'It's green. It's like—'

'It's AFS. Look! It's got it painted on the petrol tank.'

'Like that girl's.'

'Yeah.' Josie didn't go any deeper. 'Well, we can't sell this, can we? Not with a war on. We'll have to take it up the fire station.'

"Strewth, that's a long old push.'

'Then good job there's two of us.'

He gave her a look. 'Pity we can't ride it.'

'Wouldn't know how.'

'No, not me, neither. But we could have a try.'

Josie pulled the machine out from behind the rubbish. 'Listen, if anyone saw us having a ride on it, they'd think we was the ones who'd nicked it, wouldn't they? Use your loaf, Charlie.'

'More like me arms.' Charlie started pushing the handlebars of the machine, Josie behind him at the saddle.

'Not much further,' she said when they'd gone twenty

yards – which, as a laugh, didn't seem to tickle either of them.

She let Charlie stay at the front as they wheeled the bike into the school playground, and when the Station Officer was called out to see what they'd brought in, she let him do the talking.

'You say you found this?'

'Outside a scrapyard off Cable Street.'

'When?'

''S'morning.'

The officer looked them over carefully. 'It's the first you've seen of it?'

'Yup.' Charlie sounded dead honest. He could, because it was true.

'You didn't have a go on it, or anything? Yesterday?'

Charlie was a picture of innocence. 'Nope.'

So was Josie. 'On my mother's deathbed.'

The officer looked at them again, at Charlie in particular, who was small against the machine; while Josie shrank a bit.

'We thought we ought to bring it here.'

The officer walked all around the machine, like a second-hand car dealer looking for dents. 'I'm no fitter but it seems OK to me.' He called a fireman over. 'Take this to the bike bay, George. It's the missing Matchless.'

'Yes, sir.' The fireman wheeled the bike away.

'Thank you for bringing it back.' The officer still

looked suspicious, but he hadn't asked any further details of where they'd found it, so before he did, Josie marched Charlie out of the fire station, fast.

Walking indoors Josie was suddenly confronted by Ivy who was waving Liz's cap at her.

'This was sticking out under your pillow. 'Where the devil did you get it?'

'Eh? Get what?'

'This cap.' Ivy waved it at her. 'A fire girl's.'

'Oh, that. Someone give it me. Don't know where from. I said I'd take it up the fire station.'

Help! What did Ivy know? Had word got out about the UXB going up and a fire messenger getting killed – and two people riding off on her motorbike?

Ivy threw the cap onto a chair. 'Before you do anything with that you can find time to be a bit of help to me. I'm running over a new song with Fowler in twenty minutes, then I'm seeing Beattie Bassey at a friend's, and I'm getting ready for doing an Underground shelter tonight. I shan't know whether I'm on my head, my heels, or my hams.'

'Give us a chance, I'll get stuck in after dinner.'

'I'm much obliged.' And Ivy went to check her collection of shoes.

Josie swore. She should have hidden the cap better. Now she could either do what she'd said, go up to the fire station, tell them it was near where they'd found the bike, or she could just drop it somewhere. But she didn't want to do anything with it. She wanted to keep it. It was a memory of the AFS girl, and it stood for what she wanted to be herself. So she'd forget it for a while, tell Ivy she'd wait till she was going up Stepney Street sometime. If she asked.

With the bike back at the AFS the main thing now was to make sure she got to Jimmy before he came anywhere near the dock. She figured out the timing as she did the washing up. He wouldn't risk thumbing a lift off anyone, so if he'd kipped down roughly halfway from Epping it'd be this afternoon before he got close to Hermitage Quays. Then he'd most likely hole himself up somewhere on the other side of the Eastern. But no way must he get to the Western. If she wanted to see him before the war was over, or ever again even, she'd got to really put herself about to find him.

The first thing she could do was get word to everyone: use all the Dead End Kids to help look out for him. Next was what to do about Mrs Riley. Should she tell her about Jimmy's plan? Because she'd just realised what Mrs Riley could do. She could get the dock police to keep their eyes peeled for him, or even have the ship searched – which was a good idea! That would make sure he didn't go, wouldn't it?

She dried her hands. That was everything sorted in

her head – for five minutes. Because her belly gave a twist when she thought of talking to Mrs Riley. And she knew why. If she warned her about the *Gaelic Queen* it would be telling her she'd been in on the plan and helping Jimmy these last couple of days. And now Ivy knew about the AFS cap. So if the two women bumped into each other, the news of a dead AFS girl could point the finger at her and Jimmy. Ivy wasn't daft. She knew she could ride an AJS, and Mrs Riley knew Jimmy had been got out of the way somewhere. So 'A' would lead to 'B' and 'B' would lead to 'C'. Word would get out that they could have taken the bike, and she'd never be trusted as a messenger for the AFS.

No, she'd only risk the dock police knowing if everything else failed – and if necessary she'd tell them herself, long before the *Gaelic* sailed. But she hoped to hell it didn't come to that: too many questions would still get asked.

She took the cap upstairs and hid it under her mattress. She made Ivy a cup of tea and said she was going up to the school, but not to Stepney Street today.

'Where, then?'

'I'm gonna see how long it takes to walk to Addison Road. Don't want to be late for school on Monday, do I?'

'Lord forbid.'

She got one of her mother's funny looks, but she skipped out quickly – going nowhere near Addison

Road. Instead she walked to the dock gate and hung about for a while, because Jimmy had said he might come early and try something when a cart went in. But there wasn't much happening. She went to some of the Dead End Kids' houses and told them about Jimmy being in the clear – although most of them already knew. What they didn't know was the *Gaelic Queen* plan, and she wasn't saying too much about that. 'So just keep your eyes skinned.'

Next she'd go round the streets on the other side of the Eastern Dock where Jimmy might be lurking; but first she'd pop home for a cup of tea and a biscuit with Ivy, before she went off to see Auntie Beattie Bassey, let everything seem normal.

'How long, then?'

'How long what? A piece of string?' What was Ivy on about?

'How long to get to Addison Road?'

'Dunno. Haven't got a watch, have I?' She'd forgotten where she'd said she was going.

Another funny look from Ivy. 'So it was a waste of time going. You could have been…' She waved an arm at the dirty window, the heap of ironing on a chair.

'I counted my footsteps.'

'How many?'

'I've forgot exactly.' Luckily her mother was biting into her biscuit. 'But it give me a rough idea. It's like the time it takes to go up Eddie's caff.'

'And how long's that?'

'About as long as going up Addison Road.'

Ivy swallowed and choked. 'You go on like this an' they'll be coming for you in white coats, my girl. What the devil's up with you these days?'

Josie shook her head. Because there was no way she could ever tell her mother that. And meanwhile, she had to get over to the streets around the Eastern.

There was no sign of Jimmy at the Eastern or at the Western, and when the siren sounded at eight o'clock she went to the shelter with Ivy, who was going to be picked up by Freddie Fowler between half eight and nine.

These last few nights the bombing had been further off, so the shelter was getting less tense. There were more laughs, a bit of singing, the flash of playing cards, and talk was more about football and food than death and destruction – although for Josie the atmosphere could be this or it could be that, what was important was stopping Jimmy from getting into the Western. That would save a whole lot of grief.

Micky had put a railway clock on the shelter wall. Josie looked at it and worked out her timing. Whatever the Dead End Kids were doing, at half past eight she was going to hand the iron bar to Sonny and tell him she was after a short ladder she'd seen left outside a house. She'd do a good check on the streets between the London River and the Western, and then if Jimmy didn't show she'd hang about at the dock gate.

As the clock's big hand ticked round to half past she made her move with Ivy.

'They want me in a game of cribbage over the other side. If I don't see you, break a leg tonight.'

Ivy gave her funny a look; she was getting a few of those these days. 'Do my best. Be good!'

A shuffle, a sidle, a step behind the lavatory screens and out the other side – and Josie was safely in the doorway: when a sudden loud shout came down from outside.

'Fire! Fire! The stables! Bad! Elijah's horses – they're gonna go up like merry hell! Fi-i-i-ire!'

Which suddenly changed all Josie's plans.

# 19

At Tony Milner's shout she ran to the top of the stairs, stuck her head out of the blackout curtain. She could see the smoke from along the street, billowing up and masking the moon. She could hear the sounds of frightened horses, screeching and screaming in panic. Forget the London River and the Western – the *Gaelic* didn't sail till next morning, she'd got to lead her Dead End Kids to this disaster. She ran back down and did a quick and quiet round-up. 'Stable's on fire! We've got to get them horses out!'

Her crews followed her out of the shelter – to go chasing along to the stables where roof-high flames were shooting up from the bedding store at the back. Even from a distance Josie felt their heat upon her face. This needed an AFS pump and pressure hoses, widdly little stirrup pumps were useless for a fire like this. *Get Jimmy's horses out! Concentrate on that!*

'Come on!' She led her crews to the stable doors, to be baulked by Elijah pulling out a shire – a monster of a horse, bucking, snorting and steaming.

'Steady, Duke! Steady, boy!' Elijah looked around. 'Dear Lord! Someone hang onto this.' He offered the halter to anyone who'd take it, his eyes this way and that: clearly didn't know what to do with Duke but wasn't going to let him loose.

Arthur's face winced up anxiously and he bravely took the halter – and something suddenly clicked for Josie. Arthur having a wee that night in Victoria Gardens, a few yards along.

'Up the road! The park! It's got railings all round!'

Elijah pouted, then nodded. 'Get him along in the gardens,' he told Arthur. He ran back into the stables, followed by a dozen Dead End Kids.

Looking frightened out of his life, Arthur clung to the halter and ran the shire along the street, where people were coming out of the shelter to see what was happening. He took Duke into the park and in a commanding voice he ordered two women to man the gates.

Ellie came out of the stables with Prince, keeping ahead of those great hooves.

'Up the park!'

Ellie ran him fast into the gardens, where he went kicking around like a spring foal.

But what about Topper? Josie could imagine her favourite kicking and bridling in his stall, terrified of the fire. Down at the far end, he'd be one of the last to come out – and he was near to the fire, whose flames were getting a hold along the roof space.

Charlie Drew and Phil Jupp came out with a shire that threatened to run them off to Southend-on-Sea.

'Keep hold! Up the park!'

'He's too big!'

'Come on, I'll give you a hand.' Josie grabbed the horse's halter, and more off her feet than on, she helped get him into the gardens.

Now to get back for Topper. She ran back to the stables. Sonny Bailey was running Holly the Suffolk Punch to safety, followed by Elijah with two Clydesdales, and by Dougie with another. Josie turned to the sound of a fire bell clanging towards them. The AFS were here – and she was going in for Topper.

But, jeepers! Who was this, running towards her – in her dad's coat with his jumper up over his face and his cap pulled down tight?

'Jimmy! Jimmy!'

'Mother of God, look at this!'

'Jimmy! Help us! You're allowed to, you're in the clear!'

But he didn't hear. He was past her and into that blazing building without a look to left or right.

The fire engine pulled up, and a hose was run to the hydrant. The engine started its whine and within half a minute the first jet of water was hitting the flames.

Josie ran to follow Jimmy into the building, but she was hampered by Ellie coming out with Tess. Jimmy quickly followed with two smaller draughts, and Arthur and Charlie came out with two more.

Jimmy handed them over to Sonny and came face

to face with Josie. 'Topper! Is Topper out? Can't see him in there.'

'Not yet. I'm going in for him.'

'You're not. You're waiting here. He'll be needing you when I'm gone.' And he disappeared inside again. But she ignored his words and went to head in after him.

'*Josie Turner!*'

Stop! She had to turn at that voice – Ivy's, who was clicking across the street in her high heels.

'You *dare* go in there!'

Eddie came out with a carriage horse, but this was a bay, not Topper. 'Is only the white one now.'

He was followed out by Elijah. 'Knife!' he shouted at a fireman. 'Got a horse in a tangle with a rope.'

The fireman went to his belt, unclipped the studs holding his axe – as half the heavy, water-sodden roof suddenly dropped two feet in – sending up a thick wet cloud of smoke.

People screamed. A policeman tried to form a cordon on his own.

'Jimmy! Jimmy!' Josie ran for the fireman, pulled the axe from his belt, and dodged towards the stables doorway. But she was suddenly held back by the fiercest grip in Hermitage Quays. Fierce, and shaking.

'No you don't, my girl!' Ivy shouted into her face. 'You are not going in there!'

'Jimmy! Jimmy's in there!'

'I don't care if it's Jesus Christ. Look at that roof! Over my dead body are you going in!'

'I've got to!'

'No you haven't got to! This is the war. People get killed. Our Len's dead – an' while I've got life in my body you're not going, too.'

'Stand aside, miss.' The policeman was coming over to enforce Ivy's words.

'You tell her. I've lost my son to this war, and I'm not losing my daughter.' There was a loud cracking as the standing part of the building shifted a foot. 'She's a child. Get hold of her and take her down the shelter.'

'See sense, miss.' The policeman took a step nearer.

'He's my Jimmy!' Josie screamed at the pair of them. 'If he's in there, so am I!'

The grip on Josie's arm tightened even harder. 'I've turned a blind eye to some of your antics, but you're my daughter. You're my girl: you're a child.' She stared into Josie's eyes. 'Are you gonna leave me with nothing?'

Josie looked at her. Ivy was in a state, and she'd already lost enough with poor Len. But was she a child? She shut her eyes. For a moment the world seemed to stop; there were no shouts, no aircraft, no smell of smoke; it was like being under water. Was her life mud-fighting over the creek, or kissing Jimmy Riley in Epping Forest?

She felt the policeman's touch as he tried to take the axe from her hand.

'*No!*' She suddenly looked up at the sky. 'Ivy!' she screamed. 'Duck!' Everyone looked up – at nothing – as she twisted, and bent, and slipped Ivy's grip to dive into the caved-in stable and grope her way towards Jimmy.

It was dark, wet, and stinking of smoke and manure. Wood, slates and bricks were strewn all over the floor, and above her through gaps in the sagging roof she could see a searchlight glinting on a barrage balloon. Light! With her eyes stinging she pulled the torch from her pocket and shone it along the stable, but she couldn't see far for smoke. Behind her she could hear the policeman shouting.

'No one's going in!'

'Get out of my way! That's my girl in there!'

'Jimmy! Jimmy!' Josie shouted. She pulled the scarf from her neck and tied it around her mouth. But for reply all she heard was the snorting and kicking of Topper somewhere in the dark. The remains of the roof were creaking and cracking, the smoke was getting thicker, debris and water sludged under her feet – it was like being in a tunnel to some sort of hell, except it was taking her to Jimmy, and to Topper.

'Jimmy! Jimmy!' She kept close to the floor, knew that's what you had to do in a fire. What was up with him? Why wouldn't he shout back? Was he dead – choked by the smoke? Had Topper's stall caved in and crushed him? She pushed on, the axe tucked into her belt, the torch in one hand as she groped with the other. *Balance.*

And there it was – suddenly – the head of a horse in a wide-eyed panic, tossing, and coughing in great snorts. *Topper!* But where was Jimmy? She'd thought he'd be around Topper's neck, stroking him down the nose, telling him to be calm while he freed him. She shone her torch about – left, right, in front, behind her.

A cough. She shone it down. And there was Jimmy, lying under Topper's kicking hooves.

Another great creak said the roof was shifting again. Any second now this whole place was coming down. She backed herself across Topper, pushing him away and risking a bite. Now she could get to Jimmy.

'Jimmy! Jimmy!' She shook his shoulders, and saw the deep cut on his forehead.

'Jimmy!'

He coughed again and moaned. She shone the torch at Topper's fetlocks – and saw the trouble. His lead rope was too long and he'd hobbled himself. She went for the axe, but left it. Jimmy had to be first, and a hobbled Topper was better than Topper kicking him again.

'Jimmy! Jimmy! Help yourself, boy!' More people died from smoke than flames, they said, and she was choking as she breathed. For every reason they had to get out fast. With the torchlight dancing all around she got her hands under his armpits and tried to pull him up.

He groaned again, and opened one eye, then the other.

'Come on, Jimmy! Give us a hand!' She pulled again; took a deep choking breath through her scarf, and pulled once more. He was coming round, but he was still too woozy to stand. 'Come on, Jimmy, ups-a-daisy.' She pulled and lifted, and at last she got him leaning against Topper's side – which seemed to have a magical effect on the horse. He knew who it was. He quietened, and with Jimmy holding himself ready for it, she bent and gripped him round the legs to lift him again. And, praise the Lord, with a bit of weak help from him she got him lying across Topper's back, looking like a wounded cowboy.

'That's it! Hang on there!'

Jimmy coughed, moaned, spat, and lifted a hand to grip at Topper's halter. 'Good fella! Good oul Topper!' He croaked it out – and Topper calmed some more.

Josie focused her torch on the lead rope. If Topper stood still, which was only ever for a second at a time, she could just get a swing at it. But she'd have to be quick. The building was creaking louder and louder, and more slates fell in. The place was coming down on them any second.

'Talk to him, Jimmy! I've got to cut his rope.'

The axe was out of her belt and in position. She took a good grip on it. Left hand, torch. Right hand, axe. If Topper could stand still for a couple of seconds she could slice his rope in two. If she didn't... She shut her mind to the thought.

'Lovely fella! Good Topper! Top bucko!'

For a moment Topper stood calm. There were three inches of rope on the floor between his front hooves. *Now!* But he suddenly skittered; Jimmy slid about on his back and nearly came off.

'Good Topper!' He seemed to cough up his lungs. 'Bozo boy!'

Another chance – but now there were only two inches of rope to aim at. And great beams on thick bricks were rocking above them. It was now or never. Josie suddenly took the moment. She brought down the axe and sliced it through the rope.

A clean cut – but Topper had felt its wind. He jumped, cavorted, Jimmy just about clung on as Josie grabbed the rope and started pulling towards the stable's open end. And now it was as if the horse knew there was freedom ahead – or it could be Jimmy's coaxing and cajoling, reaching round between coughs and stroking him down the nose. The horse let Josie lead him on, their progress getting easier as the lights of the fire brigade showed the way towards open air.

Jimmy talked to Topper all the time – while she talked to Jimmy. 'No *Gaelic Queen* for you! No need! They all know you never done it...'

'Do they now?' But he went back to talking to Topper.

Them all getting out alive had to be the first priority.

'Father from the church told the ambulance girls. Everyone knows he told you to take the crucifix. They've signed papers.' She just about managed to cough it out.

'Good man. Good oul Father. God rest his soul.'

They were nearer to safety now, coming out through the leaning doorway to where they'd be clear. Outside, only firemen, police and civil defence were nearby, everyone else was on the other side of the street.

As they came into the open a cheer went up – stifled within seconds by a great rumbling that shook the ground and almost had Josie off her feet.

*'Jeepers! Gallop, boy!'* She pulled at the rope and Topper responded. Jimmy clung to his mane as he galloped towards the road, Josie running alongside, tripping, but somehow holding on and being dragged by the rope – clear of the building, which fell in on itself with a great crash, the final demolition.

Cheers turned to screams from across the street. *'Josie! My girl!'* The loudest voice was Ivy's.

And the softest was Jimmy's.

'That's twice, Josie Turner. Two banjaxed places almost down around my ears. What's it about when I'm some place with you?'

She pulled the scarf from her face and ducked around Topper's head to get to Jimmy. He slid off the horse's back, and she kissed him – smoky and a lot quicker than in Epping Forest. 'Dunno. But one sunny day, Jimmy Riley, some place is gonna be third time lucky for us.'

They stood there, quiet together before the world returned. Until Josie whispered, 'See you later,' and looked across at Ivy and the others, who were still held back by police. She left Jimmy and walked towards them, blew a kiss at her mother, turned her head towards Sonny and gestured for him to give her back the leader's iron bar.

'Right,' she said, in a voice loud enough for everyone to hear. 'Dead End Kids back on duty. We haven't had the All Clear yet.'

# Author's Note

This book is dedicated to the real Dead End Kids of Wapping. They carried out countless acts of bravery led by young docker Patsie Duggan (leader), Jackie Duggan, Maureen Duggan, Fred Pope, Ronnie Doyle, Harold Parker, Eddie Chusonis, Joe Storey, Terry Conelly, Graham Bath, Ronnie Eyres, Oswald Bath and Bert Eden.

Of these, Ronnie Eyres, Bert Eden and Oswald Bath were killed 'on duty' in the streets of Wapping.

The Dead End Kids' story is told in *Cockney Campaign* by Frank R. Lewey (Mayor of Stepney during the London Blitz) published by Stanley Paul and Company in 1944, more recently reproduced by Tower Hamlets Local History Library.

Bernard Ashley 2015

Read on for an extract from another thrilling
wartime story from Bernard Ashley

# Shadow of the Zeppelin

# 1

There wasn't a moon and there weren't any searchlights but there was a bit of light in the sky, and whether Freddie had heard bombs or not he couldn't remember – but something made him get up from his bed and look out, and there it was! Big, and ghostly, he could hear its engines, like some flying devil from another world. Being May it wasn't warm at night, and the sight of that thing shivered him like winter, up and down his back and round his legs. He dived into bed, pulled up the blankets and lay there scared and angry. The swines! The cowardly Huns!

They'd made life different now. Going to school was the same, so was his mother's job as a midwife, but shopping for her these days meant standing in long queues for food, and in Woolwich there was always the sight of men marching off into the army and the girls going to work in the Arsenal to make bombs and bullets. Houses and pubs were being knocked down and people were being killed and injured, although the bombs weren't dropping around their way. The papers weren't allowed to print where they fell, but up to now they didn't seem to be on this side of the river.

He knew he wasn't old enough yet, but he couldn't wait to leave school. He was on the tall side and his voice was breaking, so quite soon he could tell lies about his age. And his dad had been a boy soldier so why couldn't he be one too? Living close to the Royal Artillery at Woolwich where the gunners trained with horses and field guns, it was soldiers all around him. And if he could get to wear the khaki, wouldn't that put a firecracker up the backside of his big brother? When he wasn't at work, all Will wanted was his boater and his blazer, his lady friend, his gramophone and nights at the music hall. What he didn't want was to go to the war like loads of other boys' brothers. Now excuses for Will were running out, and it made Freddie look like a coward himself when all he wanted to do was get at those bully Germans – and get Wally Quinnell off his own back.

And the Germans needed stopping – dropping their cowardly bombs from airships onto houses and pubs and office buildings. Zeppelins, these monsters were called, and some other sort. His dad worked in the Woolwich Arsenal making shells and bullets, but when he'd been brought home ill from work his mum had packed him off over the water to Poplar to stay with a midwife friend – 'Just for a couple of days, Freddie, while I look to Dad'. The sight of that Zeppelin had scared the fly-buttons off him – and he was dead set on making his brother go and fight the Germans, stop them flying over – or his name wasn't Freddie Castle…

\* \* \*

Ernst Stender sat on his bunk at the Petty Officer's end of the crew hut and read again the letter from his wife. Rachel's words were the most loving she'd written since he'd been called-up – and nothing could ever match the thrill of what she'd kept for the end of her letter.

> *'By the way, the doctor says we will have a new mouth to feed in the summer. Yes, you are going to be a papa. Imagine our child with your dark hair and my blue eyes! From now on I shall get fatter and fatter, but you will still love me, won't you?*
>
> *I send you all my love –*
> *Mama-to-be Rachel xxx'*

He looked around the hut hoping no one had seen the look on his face. He was going to be a father! He and Rachel had been waiting for this news for some time, but his call-up had left him hoping rather than knowing. The conscription officer had persuaded him to volunteer for this coastal posting where everyone was a fighting man – no longer a boyfriend, or a husband, or a son, or a father – more a sort-of brother to everyone else in the hut. But Rachel's happy letter united him with home and it took his mind to that peaceful place: a quiet district of Berlin where he and Rachel would raise their child in tranquillity when this war was over.

Other crewmen on their bunks were reading, one of

them riffling the pages of his Bible, another deep into a thriller; one was darning a sock, while around the stove – a social centre even when it wasn't lit – a game of cards came and went in noisy bursts. But tonight everyone here would be part of the same operation, and the atmosphere was tense. He concentrated on Rachel's words as he shut out the hut to hear her voice in his head say, 'You're going to be a papa!'

He needed the courage she gave him because he was scared. But now he would be fighting for his child-to-be, too, and he'd have to be brave. What he was going to do that night was going to be done for that special person's future. Germany was at war, and he was assigned to the naval air force, rewarded with the in-between rank of Petty Officer: but why had he let himself be talked into it? Why couldn't he have been a soldier, or a real sailor on a ship? A wounded soldier with his battalion beaten would at least stand a chance of staying alive, he could lie low in a crater or a ditch; and a sailor could try to keep afloat on the wreckage of his ship. But a shot-down flying man was doomed. No parachutes were ever issued so the choice would be to jump or to crash and burn – and what sort of choice was that?

He folded his letter away as his superior Josef Porath came into the hut. The Chief Petty Officer steersman had him and Karl Klee in his team and he'd taken them both under his wing. He sat on the bed beside Ernst, the pair of them leaning forwards, heads bowed like a pair of old friends chatting: Josef bigger and tanned, Ernst pale and wiry with the build of a runner rather than a wrestler.

'I've been to a briefing,' Josef confided. 'The army Schütte-Lanz airships flew last night, tonight it's our turn.' He was a regular serviceman, a northerner with a border-country accent, who took pride in the naval service doing better than the army.

'Where are we going?' Ernst guessed it would be another sortie over the trenches of France, or an attack on a shipping lane in the North Sea.

'London.'

'*What?* We're bombing London?'

'Got to be done, got to be done – carrying more than six tons of TNT and incendiaries.' Despite the noise of the card game the hut suddenly seemed a quiet place to Ernst.

'Docks, and ordnance targets?'

'I'm not allowed to say until we're airborne.'

Ernst understood that. But his only sorties so far had been over France and the sea; he was new to the airship service but they'd picked him for compass steering because his civilian surveyor's job involved calculating distances and angles.

The naval maps showed the munitions factories at Enfield and Woolwich, as well as the string of London docks along the River Thames, so they'd find them all right. The difficulty in this humid weather was targeting any part of southern England in the midst of summer air currents and electric storms off the coast. And what had smacked everyone in the face was the crash of Zeppelin LZ10. It had frozen the blood in Ernst.

The problem had sounded almost routine at first: trouble with an engine. The telegraph operator had received a message to say the airship had fuel-supply difficulties and she wouldn't make her Nordholz base but was heading here to Hage. At this everyone was out, looking into the sky – and he'd thought he'd seen her to the north-east, hovering under a dark storm cloud. But what came next wasn't the LZ10 on a controlled approach. It was a sudden violent flash of flame and an explosion like ten racks of bombs going up.

A Zeppelin in flames was every flier's worst nightmare, and after a long wait the first eye-witness messages came in. LZ10 had been struck by lightning, a jagged flame bursting from the hull as fire engulfed her and sent her into an eighty-degree nose-dive – piling up on the tidal flats and burning to a twisted skeleton. The entire crew was lost – Lieutenant Karl Hirsch and nineteen men – but only eleven charred corpses were found in the wreckage; so the question everyone asked was, had the rest made that other terrible choice and jumped – their bodies lost at sea?

That accident had paralysed his nerve; but Josef had fallen in next to him, walking the flat grass of Hage. 'Put it away, put it away; of course accidents happen.'

'I thought they said fire can't spread inside a Zeppelin skin. It's not as if it's one big hydrogen balloon.' Ernst had counted the sixteen separate cells in their own airship and he knew that if one cell got hit the gas would disperse in the outer envelope. 'That's what they say, isn't it?'

Josef took longer strides than he did and he'd got ahead; now he stopped and lit them both a cigarette. 'Pressure height, Ernst, that's what did it for them, that's where Hirsch was unlucky. His ship got above pressure height, and all her cells started valving gas into the envelope – just as the lightning struck.' Josef put his fingers to his small moustache as if he were adjusting it. 'But with the help of the Lord God, Mathy won't make a mistake like that.'

What Josef had said was like a good friend's arm around his shoulder. A captain with Lieutenant Mathy's reputation would surely keep his airship under the pressure height, wouldn't he? Although that wasn't the only thing that could affect them. They were also in the hands of the weather, and the physics of flight, and of luck, too, as it struck both sides. But one thing was clear in Ernst's mind: help from Josef's Lord God didn't come into things. War on earth was made and its winners were decided by what men did.